ENDANGERED

You are the difference!

Kian Sabik

You are the difference!

Kian Sabih

ENDANGERED

KIAN SABIK

Endangered

This book is a work of historical fiction. Apart from well-known real people, events and places, all names, places and incidents in the narrative are products of the author's imagination or are used fictionally. Any resemblance to current events or living people is entirely coincidental.

Cover Design: Ebook Launch Covers
Map Credit: Mapswire.com

ISBNs:
979-8-9866864-0-0 (Ebook)
979-8-9866864-1-7 (Paperback)
979-8-9866864-2-4 (Hardcover)

First Edition: August 2022

10 9 8 7 6 5 4 3 2 1

GLOSSARY

Bèndàn - Idiot

Gǒu - Dog

Háizi - Child

Lǎolao - Grandmother

Lǎoshī - Teacher

Móguǐ - Devil

Núlì - Slaves

Pàntú - Traitor

Wēi wú ěr réng - Uyghur

Xíngshì - Brat

Yě shòu - Beast

Yěmán rén - Barbarians

Zuìfàn - Criminal

Please note that the words under the chapter numbers are numbers in the Uyghur language

ÜRKESH

XINJIANG NOW

1

BIR

IMAGINE BEING TIED to a tiger chair, your hands and feet shackled in an agonizing position. Now imagine sitting in that position for hours and hours, unable to move, your muscles aching. Or imagine having wires attached to your body, electricity shooting through your blood. Or being dunked in ice-cold water, only coming up for a few seconds until you wish you could die.

Maybe you're thinking about the Holocaust, or perhaps you believe this is all fiction. That it's a new "trend" or a slander. Maybe you just don't care because why would you care about what's happening on the other side of the globe?

But this is exactly what we go through in the concentration camps of the hunters.

To all of us, the hunters are the same. The same dictators. The same tyrants. The same haters.

They are the Chinese government.

But who are we?

In their eyes, we are barbarians, tortured and killed at their desire. We are ghosts whom nobody sees. We are puppets, controlled by their strings. They believe we are savages just because we believe in something different. Something they deem as "wrong."

But they forgot that we are humans like them. They forgot that we feel pain. That we-

"Ürkesh. Hala. Time to eat."

I jump, rip the page out and crumple it into a ball.

You could get into serious trouble if anyone ever reads this. And you thought you could bury this somewhere and that someone in the future would find it and remember you? No one will ever find it. It's hopeless.

I dart down the hallway, the paper ball bouncing in my pocket until I reach the kitchen. After scanning the room, I light the tip of the paper on fire and toss it into the sink.

Hssss.

The water transforms into steam as it touches the crumpling, black paper. I watch the ashes float into the drain just as the little plant of hope in my heart melts away.

“Ürkesh, where are you?” Mama asks from the living room.

“I’m right here,” I mumble.

“Come and eat dinner.”

An image of dinner pops into my head.

A dry,

bland,

And a nearly empty bowl.

"Dinner" does not even begin to describe the meal. The little contents of the bowl do nothing to quell the beast in my stomach. It growls for fresh bread,

For warming soup,

For tender meat,

For juicy fruit,

But those luxuries rarely come. There's hardly any food in our cupboards and the stove begs to be used. Papa's laborious work provides us with nothing but vegetables every day. Anything more than that comes at the expense of barely eating anything all day.

"Ürkesh, is something wrong?" Mama asks as I shuffle out of the kitchen. Her wrinkleless face shines and her deep, dark, gentle eyes pull mine into a trance.

"No."

"Why the sad face then?"

"Nothing."

I’m just tired of eating the same thing every single day. I’m tired of having no way out.

"Well, *something's* wrong. You can't hide it from me. I'm your mom, in case you forgot," she grins.

A baby smile spreads on my face.

"Come on, tell me," she pauses, "is it the salad?"

"Maybe."

A look of sadness reflects in her eyes. "Listen, Ürkesh. I know you are tired of vegetables but don't think about it. This is better than having nothing at all. Now, turn that frown into a smile and be grateful that you have at least some food. There are many kids out there that don't have anything to eat at all. They resort to garbage, which tastes worse than what's in front of you. Sometimes, they can't find trash, so they starve to death. You know that so reflect on it. Salad is better than starvation so be grateful, my dear child."

"Yes, Mama."

I sit on the floor, forcing the dry, bland greens down my throat. Papa begins talking about work and everyone leans in to listen. Soon, everyone's plates are empty.

Except mine.

I must return to my room before Mama makes me wash the dishes and clean up. But she'll never let me unless I have a valid excuse.

Suddenly, a light bulb flashes above my head.

My homework.

I need to get to my homework.

It's like a faraway treasure on a mountain surrounded by green snow I must devour to reach the summit. I *must* get to the peak as fast as I can.

I down all the greens and bolt up the stairs.

"Ürkesh, where are you going in such a hurry?" Papa asks.

"I'vegottofinishmyhomework." The heavy wooden door slams shut behind me and I spy the stack of books with paper climbing it. There's the treasure I've worked so hard for.

"HOW DID I see this as gold?" I mutter under my breath. My one-hundred-pound eyelids fight to close.

Yawn.

Tick.

Don't sleep...

Tock.

Almost done...

Tick.

Last question...

Tock.

Hala gently snores in the corner as I float to the kitchen.

11:18 p.m. Waaaaay past bedtime.

Go...to...sleep...

I squish myself against the wall and walk sideways, avoiding the screaming floorboards.

Creeeeeeeeak.

"Mmmmh...Ürkesh?"

I freeze.

"Yes?"

"Why are you awake? It's like two a.m."

"Don't worry. It's not even close to two. It's not my fault. I was completing homework that's due *tomorrow.* You won't understand until you're my age. I'm going to sleep now."

"You should have done your assignment earlier. Good night."

I don't respond. This has been my routine for a very long time now. It's not that I hate her. I just don't have the time. I have school in the morning and homework when I come back. Factoring in time with my friend, chores, sleep and showers, I simply don't have the time to sit and play make-believe with her. She's also thirteen while I'm sixteen. That's a huge age difference. I don't do the things she does. I'm not a child and I'm not a girl. She's also *very* annoying, the *most* annoying sister in the entire world.

"Ürkesh, why don't you respond to me anymore? I haven't done anything wrong. Ürkesh? Ürkesh? Hello? You're ignoring me. I know you're not asleep. You never fall asleep that fast. Come on, Ürkesh."

I lock my eyes shut and suck in air greedily, inhaling and exhaling like a mountain. She can't know I'm pretending. She's still a child.

CHATTER FLOATS AROUND in the still, humid air. Wild laughing piles on top of words, puncturing holes in the ears of onlookers. Curious eyes peek at the forbidden desk. Others quietly complain about the school, their eyes searching the room for an adult.

Crrrrrr.

The door squeaks open as Mr. Gao walks into the classroom and makes his way toward his desk. Everyone shuffles around and stands in front of their seat.

“Good morning, class,” he announces.

“Good morning, *Lǎoshī*,” we bow and reply.

“As I mentioned on Friday, you all have your Unit Five test today. I hope to see you all score in the high nineties. Now, hand me your assignments.”

Whoosh. Whoosh.

Each paper glides into the waiting teacher's hand until he reaches my chair.

"Kai, where is your homework?"

"It's here, sir. Let me get it."

A searching hand rummages through my backpack.

Where is it? I finished it last night. It should be right here.

A desperate whimper escapes my lips.

"Did you complete your work?"

"I...I thought I did. I was tired last night, so I only finished half of it. I'm sorry, sir."

A few smirks spread on the student's faces as the creases wrinkle on Mr. Gao's leathery face. Fingers go up to rub his eyebrows as a tight, irritated frown crumples his blank expression.

"I'm really sorry, sir."

"I'm disappointed with you, Kai. Come to my desk after the bell rings."

"Wéi wú ĕr réng."

"Bèndàn."

"He's going to kill you just like you deserve."

"Enough, everyone. If I hear one more word, I will make you fail. I'll be passing out the test now. I want you to begin immediately and once you're done, put it in this bin."

Kreeeeeee.

A sharp, piercing ringing echoes throughout the school. Everyone swarms through the door, talking and laughing until there's only one person left.

I drag my feet to Mr. Gao's desk, bracing myself for whatever he throws at me.

"Kai, I'm extremely disappointed with you. You let your laziness take control of you. I'm afraid I can't let this go. Consequently, you have to complete double the amount of work in two days. Here you go," Mr. Gao scolds. He reaches into a drawer and dumps twenty sheets into my hands.

"Double?" My hand slaps my mouth.

"I see you're not satisfied with double," he drops another ten papers, "Now, it's triple. You are dismissed."

I turn towards the door.

"Oh, Kai? Here's a letter to your parents as well. Tell them that I would like a reply by Monday."

"Thank you, sir. Have a great day," I force out, exiting the near-empty building.

"Hi, Mama," I groan when the door screams open.

"Hi, Ürkesh. How was school?"

"Fine."

"Just 'fine'?" Her eyes land on the paper in my hands, "What's that?"

I shove the paper into her arms. Her eyes glide over the words.

"That explains it. Ürkesh, look at me." I look at her thoughtful, smiling face, "Don't waste any more time. Go complete the rest of your homework and don't worry about it. Everyone makes mistakes and besides, it's your first time. It's happened to me before...more than once."

"Really?"

"Yes, but we're not going to talk about that. Anyway, hurry up. You have a lot to do. Remember to pray."

"Yes, Mama. Thank you for understanding, Mama. Don't worry, this will never happen again."

"I love you, Ürkesh."

"I love you too, Mama."

I really, really do.

Aaaaah.

"Mama? Papa? Hala? Does anyone else hear that?"

Only the ghostly silence responds.

TAP. TAP.

"Open the door. Open the door. Help. Help. *Help.*"

The door handle whimpers as my trembling hand fidgets with it.

Open up.

"Aaaaaaah."

Thump.

I peer through the crack and my eyes beg to go back inside. A stick-like boy lays crumpled on the front steps. His deep blue eyes stare upwards and his spiky hair springs messily from his head.

My head throbs.

My heart races.

My blood freezes.

Yu. Yu is dead. The police got him. They killed him. My best friend is...

Dead.

2

IKKI

“KAI? KAI. KAI. You can wake up now."

What happened? Why is Yu awake? Wasn't he dead a few minutes ago? Am I dead? Are we both dead?

Ha, ha, ha.

"You're...laughing...*why?*"

That's what flips the switch. Yu begins rolling on the floor like a hysterical, insane man, trying to suck in air.

A realization hits me like a drummer hitting a gong. "You were playing a prank on me, weren't you? Is that why you're laughing so hard?"

"Relax, Kai. It was a joke."

"A *joke*? Pretending to die is a *joke*? Causing others to faint is just a prank? *You* and your *pranks,*" I look around and lean into his ear, "You know anything can happen in this country. You know that you could've been killed in a *split second."*

"Calm down. If I knew you would explode like that."

"Well, you should've known *I would explode like that.* You understand me. We're friends. Friends don't play these kinds of pranks. I could've *died."*

"Friends don't erupt on something so small. We're not even friends; we're best friends. Come on, Kai. Forgive and forget."

Mr. Gao didn't "forgive and forget." My extra homework didn't "forgive and forget." The control I had on the switch evaporates and it bursts into flames. My mind short-circuits and my heart races.

"Forgive and forget? We both know the situation we're living in and yet you still have to do these irritating pranks. No wonder no one else wants to be your friend. Believe me, because I've *tried.* No wonder the bullies always pick on you because *you deserve it."*

Yu's mouth hangs open a little to show the black and white inside and his eyes flood.

The flames extinguish as a single tear drips down his face.

"Yu...I'm so sorry. I didn't mean it. I was...irritated. I'm sorry."

His face darkens. "Ha, you're *sorry*. You're sorry after saying so many hurtful things. And you were *irritated*. You call that irritation? That is not irritation; it's anger. I don't want to spend time with someone who takes everything too seriously."

The lava seeps out of the volcano. The Earth trembles as each tremor stops its heart.

So this is all my fault? It's my fault that I fainted because I cared about him?

"Fine. I don't care if you leave or not. I don't even care if you're my friend. I don't need anyone, let alone you."

I stomp into the house, a thunderstorm brewing behind me.

"-need to do something. This is serious," Papa begs.

"What can we do, Ismail? Absolutely nothing," Mama says.

I come out from behind the hall. "What's wrong?" I ask.

Papa rubs his forehead. "I was at work and overheard a conversation between two coworkers."

I wait for him to continue but only silence greets me. "What were they talking about?"

"It's nothing, Ürkesh."

"It's alright, Ismail. He's not a child anymore. He should know." Mama squeezes his shoulder.

"My coworkers were talking about the new crackdown the government has started. They've expanded their camps and are now detaining anyone who wears a scarf, grows a beard, prays or says anything in Arabic. They're passing a law banning Islam. They think we're terrorists.

"It's not the people's fault; it's the government's. They're using propaganda to brainwash their citizens. The people don't know anything about us. I know they wouldn't stand with the Communist Party if they did.

"I'm afraid for our lives. We need to do something just in case they come for us."

"Like what? We can't hide from the government," I remark.

Papa's eyes light up. "I know exactly what we could do."

NIGHT STRIKES LIKE a raid. Deafening silence runs through the village. The stiff air sinks, roaming the land like a wolf. A blanket of complete black falls onto us.

"We only have a few hours to dump as many necessities under the trapdoor as we can," Papa whispers as if these are his last words. Back and forth, we dump cans, bottles, batteries, flashlights and so much more into the black hole in the middle of our living room. It's as if a train plummeted through the floor, never to be found again.

I can see it all right here.

The bullets, the screams, the crying.

The smell of rotting eggs, urine and blood all mixed to form the sharp stench of death.

The cracking of bones, the rattling of chains and the splash of blood.

Everything plays before my eyes until a ghostly, painful silence floats down.

KNOCK. KNOCK.

Our muscles freeze, all eyes turn toward Papa. A sparkling drop drips down the side of his face. He tiptoes his way to the door and peeps through a crack. A heavy breath exits his lungs.

"Shan, come in," Papa exclaims, a little surprise bouncing in his voice.

He plays with his fingers as a menacing, towering man stomps through the house. His dark hair flows over his shoulders and a bright orange roll sticks out of his mouth. His bushy eyebrows furrow together, forming a gray line on his forehead. No wonder everyone hides from him. They think he's a thief or part of a gang and he does look the part.

Crash.

"Why is your ceiling so low," he growls, the fangs glistening in his mouth.

"I can't control that. I'm sorry," a hushed Papa responds.

Crack.

A faint glow explodes on the cigarette in Uncle's mouth.

Uhhhhua.

Hala wheezes as he blows the smoke right into her face. His deep, booming laughter echoes in the house as she rushes to breathe clean, clear air. I latch to her arm and pull her into our room.

"Why did you do that?"

"I don't want Uncle to hurt us."

"He's our *uncle*. He's family. He can't harm us even if he wanted to."

“Please, stay here. Let Mama and Papa deal with him."

"Deal with him? Ürkesh, he's family. No one is closer and more trustworthy than family. If we can let Yu into our house, we can also let Uncle in."

"Yu’s a different case. Uncle visits us once every few years. He doesn’t even care about his own sister."

"He's not. Just because he's your friend doesn't mean he can come in. Shan is our uncle so he's closer than a friend. He has more of a right to enter our house. Besides, Papa wouldn't have let him in if he was dangerous."

"Why can't you just listen?" My hand curls tighter around her arm.

"Let me go. You're hurting me."

"No. You're going to stay here whether you like it or not. I'm your older brother. I know more about this stuff than you do so listen. This is for your own good."

"Let. Me. Go." She twists and turns my arm until I howl in pain. Slow tears trickle down her face while a storm brews above her head.

"Why can't you be kind to your sister?"

"I'm sorry, Mama."

Mama holds Hala tight, running her hands through her hair.

"Don't apologize to me. Sorry is not enough, especially if you don't act upon it. Treat Hala like she's your best friend because she is and should be. The best people are those best to their families. You can't be polite and well-mannered in front of outsiders and then bully your sister at home. That is not what our religion teaches us. We must be the best people we can be behind and in front of others. Be grateful that Allah has blessed you with a friend who lives with you."

"I'm sorry, Hala. I won't do it again."

"Are you sure you won't, Ürkesh?" Mama asks, the steel evident in her voice.

"Ye-"

Whoooosh.

The door bursts open as a disheveled, panting Papa bursts through it. "They're coming. The police are all over town. They're searching every house. We need to get in the hideout *now.*"

CRASH. THUD. THUD.

"Search the house and don't leave a single bed upturned. Don't damage anything valuable," a stern, deep voice commands, the smirk on his face echoing through his voice.

A dark, chilling fog sinks, swallowing the still air. Terror creeps into my heart and courses through my veins, slowly paralyzing me. An unsettling silence pierces through the air, ringing.

Tick.

Tock.

Tick.

Tock.

Until a storm erupts.

Glass shatters.

Dust rains.

Walls tremble.

My eyes catch Papa wrapping his arm around Mama. Her bright face is now bleached, white as a ghost.

"Sir, no one's in the house."

"We can't waste time waiting for them. We'll come back tomorrow when they're here. Life would have been easier for them if they'd only been here. Let's move."

Papa leans down and whispers something in Mama's ear. She leans into him and closes her eyes, a worried frown glued to her face.

The resonating footsteps become hushed tiptoes and then silence. Our tensed muscles beg to breathe, but the looming threat above shushes them until the blanket of sleep finally wraps us up and pulls us into its deep spell.

3

ÜCH

"ÜRKESH. ÜRKESH. Get up," a hushed voice peeps. My blurred vision clears up to find a tear-stricken face staring into my eyes.

"What?"

No answer.

"Is something wrong? Hala, is something wrong?"

No answer.

"Come on, Hala. You couldn't have woken me up for no reason. That's not possible. Don't do this to me. *What's wrong?"*

My ears take in the complete silence.

"Mama and Papa."

My eyes dart to where they usually sleep, only to find the barren, dusty floor and a pile of crumpled blankets. A sliver of light peeks through the crack from the barely open trapdoor.

"Where? Where are they? Hala, where are they?"

"They're gone. I heard it all."

"Where?"

"The soldiers took them."Everything becomes a blur. *"Where are they? Where? Where? Tell me."*

"Ürkesh. Ürkesh. *Ürkesh."*

"What?"

"Stop. Stop. Please stop. Yelling won't help."

The anger slowly stops bubbling as realization climbs into my heart. The air finally bursts out of my lungs as my heart stops beating crazily.

"I'm sorry, Hala. I'm sorry."

"We need to *go*. We need to leave. We need to leave China," she whispers.

“But what about...them?” My eyes point to where our parents were.

“I don’t think they’re coming back.”

I nod, a sinking feeling wiggling in my stomach.

Creeeeeeeeeeeak.

The trapdoor screams, trying to warn the soldiers. The wood laughs at our attempt to run. The solid door tries to push us back into the house but ultimately fails.

Thud. Thud.

"Ürkesh, look."

I shove Hala into an alleyway, pulling myself along with her, away from the roaming lions. Cramped behind moldy crates, silent prayers escape my lips.

Drip.

Anticipation falls down like drops of water. The air stops in my throat with the incoming earthquakes, trying to free itself from the closing prison.

Drip. Drip.

Muffled whimpers slip from Hala's mouth as each second brings the soldiers closer and closer.

Dripdripdripdripdrip.

"Should we check this place?" a mouse-like voice squeaks.

"Nah, no one could've gotten in there, especially not on my watch. Besides, I'm hungry. Let's go. Our shift is almost over and I can't wait to go back home. I can't stand this cold, dark place anymore."

After what seems like a day, I peer out from the alley.

"Hey. What are you kids doing out here?" A dark figure waves at us.

"Hala, don't say a word to him," I whisper.

Yu used to make fun of me for looking Han. If he thought that, the guard could too.

The guard's eyes comb us once he arrives. "Where are your parents, child?"

"They died a long time ago, sir."

"Hmm...how old are you?" The man shoots daggers into my eyes as if reading my thoughts. I heap my courage from the pit of my stomach.

"I'm eighteen, sir."

"And who's the girl with you?"

"She's my younger sister."

"How old is *she?"*

"Thirteen, sir."

"What are you doing here? Don't you know the Uyghurs live here?"

"I didn't know until I got here. We immediately got out of the town to avoid those barbaric creatures." Hala's eyes dart towards mine and I fight the urge to look back.

"Ah, so you are pure Han Chinese?"

"Sir. What did you think I was? Did you confuse me for those filthy animals?"

Hala's eyes widen and she tries to hide them from the man.

"My apologies. I assumed you were Uyghurs. If I were you, I'd stay *far* away. The government is detaining thousands of Uyghur and they might mistake you as one if they see you in any of their towns. They won't care about anything if they catch you," He leans in, "You wouldn't want to be in those horrific camps."

"Thank you, sir. I shall take your advice very seriously." I bow, spin and walk in the opposite direction.

I try to keep the courage in my heart as we walk out of the town's border. I don't even look back to mourn my hometown. I can't. Not with the police swarming all over the place.

Whooooosh.

A numbing, icy wind blows right through me, chilling my bones.

Clack. Clack.

My teeth clatter together as the cold climbs higher and higher.

Crunch. Crunch.

The dead grass and fallen leaves crumple underneath my feet, each crunch sending my heart fluttering.

The weather is like the government's heart. All the warmth has evaporated. Everyone's hearts have turned hard and cold like an everlasting winter. No one has any compassion left. This is the kind of world we're living in now.

As we inch towards a tree, I pile branches into my arms and within seconds of rubbing two sticks together, orangish-yellow sparks come to life.

Crackle. Crack.

The fire tries to reach the sky and the firewood dances until it dies. The orange battles with the white in an everlasting and deadly engagement. The sky cracks open and light escapes from its wound. The dark clouds hurry to close the gap as our eyes close and our minds float to the clouds.

"KAI? Is that you?"

"Huh?"

I cover my eyes as the blinding sun glares down at me. Bare trees wave in the wind and a few dead leaves dance. Only the white, gray and brown of winter greet me.

"Am I dead?"

A dirty, worried face appears before me. "Kai, stop it."

"Yu."

I squeeze my dear friend into a warm hug. "I'm so sorry for getting angry the other day. I didn't mean any of it. I *do* care about our friendship. I'm really sorry."

"It's fine. You were angry. Besides, we have a much, much bigger problem on our hands. How did you guys come all the way here? Weren't you...safe in your hideout?"

"We were."

I tell him *everything.*

The soldiers.

Mama and Papa.

Escaping.

Everything.

"What about you? How did you escape?"

Panic flashes on his face. But as soon as it comes, it disappears, sadness replacing it.

"I was out buying some vegetables when the screaming began. The grocer hid me under his stall and covered me so the soldiers wouldn't find me. But he...he was caught, and he tried to fight. The men beat him until he was unconscious. I must have stayed under the stall for hours because when I came out, the market was deserted. I ran home to find...to...to find Mama and Papa..."

A lone tear streams down his face.

Silence.

I know the rest of the story. I reach out and squeeze his shoulder.

"Well, I'm glad we found each other. Safety in numbers, right?" he croaks and tries to smile.

I nod.

Grrrrrr.

"Yu, is that your...*stomach* or a bear?"

The sadness on Yu's face is replaced by embarrassment.

"Sorry. I guess I'm really, really hungry. We should probably look for food before I scare all the animals away," he smiles nervously, "Wake Hala up."

"Hala, wake up. We've got to go for a while," I whisper. No answer. "Hala. Hala. *Hala.* Get up."

Her eyelids crack open a little. "Leave me alone."

"Hala, come on."

"Why?"

"We have to look for food before nightfall. You don't want to starve, right? Come on."

Khaaa. Khaaaa.

Gentle snores fill the air as Hala and Yu sleep next to the fire. Sleep has left me like a soul leaving a body. I sit up, watching the moon spy on us.

"Why can't life be easier?" The words spill out. "We can't trust anyone. The government is coming to send us to our deaths. They aren't sending us to 're-education camps.' They are forcing us into concentration camps. Does anyone even understand what that means? They are throwing us into camps where we will be tortured and beaten mercilessly. If torture doesn't kill us, the Chinese will murder us with their own hands. Hasn't the world learned its lesson during the Holocaust?"

The moon stares, its face turning a ghastly white. Holes form from the fear and its eyes freeze from the horror. It tries to say something but it can't. No one can.

The cold decides to take a nap from its torment. "Who...Who are you?"

"Shhhhh."

A form wraps a dark, heavy blanket around me. "What are you doing?"

"Shhhh."

MY EYES FLUTTER open to the blinding sun. The leaves dance in the wind and the grass laughs. The animals climb higher and higher to witness the majesty of the frozen forest. Sparkles from the tips of branches wink and a light stream of smoke claws at the sky in an attempt to break free.

"Yu, do you see that? We're not alone. What if it's a Chinese encampment? What if it's someone loyal to the Han? No sane Uyghur would light a fire when there could be soldiers here."

"Ürkesh, calm down. Please. That's just an old lady. She gives me food when I can't find any. I mean, I've only gone to her once and she did give me a lot of food...but still. We need that kind of food to live. Don't stop us from going to her. *Please.* What can an old lady do to us anyway? She's so old, she can hardly walk. It's not like she can shoot us down with a rifle. We're going to die without that food."

"But she can call the police here."

"It's a desolate area. There's no connection here and it would take her ages to physically get anywhere where there is a signal. She doesn't even know where we live, not that we have a home or anything. I don't want to starve to death. *Please?*"

I want to trust Yu but I can't. A gnawing monster bites at my insides. *What if this woman is willing to give us up to the police? What if she's willing to strangle us with her bare hands?*

Grrrrrrr.

My stomach joins Yu and begs for food.

"Fine. Let's go."

Knock. Knock.

A tiny woman appears at the door. Her snow-white hair glistens in the sunlight and the wrinkles on her face droop toward the Earth. Huge, dark circles encompass her eyes and when she smiles, it's all black inside. She pulls us inside and hugs Yu. "Who are these two?"

"These are my friends, Kai and An."

"Come on in. You three must be hungry."

I vigilantly inspect the humble cottage. A fire lights the house and only a mattress and food call this place home. All the fear drips down onto the floor and is replaced by security.

"I'm going to go get some dry sticks from the forest. You guys stay here and make yourself at home. Feel free to use or eat anything," *Lǎolao* offers before leaving.

We wait and wait, playing some games and having a good time. *Lǎolao* comes back after fifteen minutes with a few sticks piled into her sagging arms and tosses them in the fireplace, the orange licking them. She dumps meat, onions, vegetables and spices in the pot, a livening smell floating out of it and tickling our noses.

She hands us a bowl filled with the liquid to the brim and we gulp it down. The warm soup fills me with a new, intense energy.

"Do you like it?"

"That. Was. The. Best. Soup. Ever," Hala exclaims.

“I’m glad to hear that.” A tired, wrinkled smile forms on Hua's face. "It's time for my nap but you children are welcome here whenever you want."

"Thank you, *Lǎolao*. I haven’t eaten anything like this in ages. The soup was delicious," I say, the broth warming my insides.

Hua nods and constantly glances at the window.

Slam.

The instant we all step out of the cottage, the door slams shut behind us. My blood turns into ice. It's like she wanted to get rid of us.

"Did you noti-"

"Halt."

A large, metal object jams into my side. Yu and Hala's faces drain, turning into a ghostly white. They stand there, staring into the unknown, their eyes frozen. I gulp and turn around to peer into the face of a Chinese soldier, his gun buried into my side.

4

TÖT

"DON'T. MOVE."

An ancient face peers from the door.

Lǎolao.

She must have told them we're here. She didn't go to get firewood. She went to report us. It doesn't take that long to gather sticks. I knew it. We shouldn't have trusted her. I shouldn't have listened to Yu. I should have listened to my gut.

A soldier grabs a flooding pouch and hands it to the old woman.

They're paying her. They're paying her for reporting us.

A shudder escapes my lips.

My eyes focus on the gun, making sure it doesn't rip a hole through my side. Silent tears drip down Hala's face onto the dead snow, the gentle drips turning into ice. Yu stares into nothing, dazed as if he is seeing angels.

Like a bolt of lightning, I snatch Hala's hand and tug until the trees become nothing but blurs.

Tetetetetetetetetete.

Bullets rain down.

Time slows down.

Commands crash down.

Dodging a shocked branch, we turn onto an abandoned pathway. My heart pounds like crazy saying,

Run.

Run.

Run.

A piercing scream comes from behind me.

Time stops.

The barking stops.

The bullets stop.

Silence.

Crimson.

The ground greedily drinks the thick, red liquid and the color from Hala's face leaks. A waterfall of blood flows out of her calf, her leg drowning in the lake of blood. One soldier, then another and then another come into sight and form a circle around us, their loaded guns laughing in our faces.

Hatred dances in my eyes. They shot my sister. No one gets away with hurting *my sister*.

"Young man, if you are intelligent, you won't run again," a tall, muscular man warns. He looks like all the other Han soldiers except for the deep scar running down his face.

"If you were intelligent, you would leave us alone," I snap back like a rabid dog.

"Control your tongue, *Yě shòu*. I am *your* superior."

"Says the one who is calling me terrible things. Control *your* tongue."

The air stops filling my lungs and my feet can't feel the ground. "You're a sharp one, huh? I have a special *procedure* for sharp ones. I'll have fun with you."

"Soldiers, lower your weapons and *you*, drop the boy."

An elderly man appears from the forest. Even though he looks like he's eighty, his body is like that of a thirty-year-old.

I back farther and farther away until my hands find nothing but the air. I flip over to see a drop-off. Now, we're really cornered unless...

"Trust me," I whisper into Hala's ear.

I scooch as close to the end as possible.

"What are yo-"

The air lets go. I hang in the air, eyes shut, waiting for the *crash* but it never comes. My eyes open to the "superior" holding my wrist.

There goes that idea.

"What. Were. You. Thinking?" Drops of spit spray onto my face.

"Enough. How many times have I told you all not to hurt them? *You're* the reason he attempted to fall off the cliff. He would never have tried to do that if you had been gentle with him. Now you, you and you go search the area for more. You, stay here with me," the commander barks. The men's eyes burn as they force their feet to go in the other direction.

As soon as they're all gone, the man kneels and wraps a white cloth around Hala's leg. "I'm sorry, *Háizi.* My men, they are a bunch of animals. They love to use their weapons. I have told them so many times, but they don't listen. *Please,* don't try to run again. I'm afraid I won't be able to stop them next time."

"Why are you being so nice to us?" I ask before covering my mouth.

"I don't think what's going on is right. It's genocide. Just because someone believes in something different or doesn't look Chinese doesn't mean they deserve to die."

"Why won't you do something? Why won't you let us go?"

"I've tried but it all went wrong. They killed him. I can't do it again. I can't have another person's blood on my hands. Now, let's go before there's any more trouble."

A cry pops out of Hala's mouth as I scoop her up.

"I'm sorry," I whisper.

She continues whimpering as if she didn't even hear me. After a few minutes, a shadowy van appears. It cackles in delight and devours us in one bite. All the light evaporates and only the darkness remains.

Silent, empty darkness.

Yu is already there, his face lowered, trying to hide the wet streaks on his cheeks. Hala begins weeping in the dark and I try to comfort her.

The problem is, I'm not great at making others feel better. I've never had to comfort anyone like this. That was always Mama and Papa's job. Yu stares at the wall, his eyes hollow of any life. His mouth slightly drops to reveal the pearls inside.

"Snap out of it."

"There is no hope now. We're *all* going to die."

"We have to fight if we want a chance."

"We don't have a chance."

"We do as long as we fight. We can't give in."

Not a single word comes out of our mouths for the rest of the hours-long drive. Yu swims in his thoughts while Hala drowns in her tears. Me, I do nothing but wait.

Wait.

Wait.

And wait.

For our imminent deaths.

5

BESH

"WELCOME TO YOUR new home," the "superior" says.

A home is supposed to be a place where there is the love and light of a family.

A place where there is happiness and laughter.

A place where there is peace and comfort.

Not where there is coldness,

Pain,

And screaming.

I look at Hala, then Yu and at the camp entrance. Blood red letters glare at me.

Welcome.

My heart beats faster and faster as the word cackles

You.

Can.

Never.

Run.

Away.

From.

Me.

"How long does it take to get out?" a guard barks.

I scoop Hala up as the weight in my heart drags me farther into the sea of despair.

"Hey, *get back in there."*

"Isn't this our stop?"

"It's the girl's. You both are going to a *different* re-education facility."

"Why?"

Slap.

A bolt of lightning reaches out and a clap of thunder booms, laughing. I can feel the red on my face and his hand permanently imprinted onto my cheek.

"Does that answer your question?"

My anger pulls me up until my eyes bear into his.

"Kai, *don't,"* Yu warns. He grips my arm, holding me back.

His words fall on deaf ears. I continue glaring, my teeth grinding against each other. I can see the fire in his eyes and the smoke in his ears.

But I still stare.

And stare.

I stare until rage tugs at my heart.

"Why can't you be someone other than a killer?" I blurt.

Astonishment pulls open his eyes and the hatred seethes. It seethes out of him, branding me all over. His head rises higher than the mountains.

"I'm only protecting my country from the likes of you."

"Or are you just serving your desires?"

"Shut. Up. Get into the car before I kill you *and* your sister."

The man tears Hala from me.

"Stop it," I demand.

"Make me."

"Stop it. She's coming with me."

" Take her from me. I dare you. *Take her."*

He dangles Hala in front of me.

All I can see is red. Red, boiling, blinding blood. The ground underneath me melts away and I soar above them all until I explode onto him. My clenched hands pound, deafening *thuds* echoing through the air. I tear the life from him. I tear at his arrogance, pride, sight, heart, everything. Bees swarm all around, their *bzzzzzz* tearing my mind. More and more swarm around me. My ears pound, the *thump, thump* echoing. They sting and sting without any mercy. Without any compassion. Without any pity. Like savage creatures with no respect for human life.

Within seconds, the man isn't underneath me anymore. Hala isn't there anymore either. My starved eyes search the entire perimeter until I spy a thrashing, injured deer struggling in the jaws of a ruthless tiger.

"Stop. Stop. Stop. Stop. Stop. Stop. Stop. *Stopstopstopstop."*

Instantaneously, my hands and feet turn into hooves and keen, thick horns erupt from my head. The ground is but a dark blur as the man grows closer and closer, the fire in his eyes dancing and the hot smoke rising from his nose. I can get him. I can reach him. Until time stops and I freeze in the air, the bees blocking my path. Millions of hands pull me back further into the darkness, their thorns stabbing me everywhere.

"Move. Move. Move!"

I shove the wave away. I flap my arms wildly against the swarm of bees but only fiery stings respond.

"Ürkesh. Ürkesh. Ürkesh. Ürkesh. *Ürkesh. Ürkesh."*

No one even turns around. No one listens. No one hears my screams,

My pleas.

My tears.

Rain floods down. Storm clouds wrap around the sun, preventing it from shining. Everything becomes blurred as reality chokes me.

Hala's gone.

Hala's gone.

Hala's gone.

6

ALTE

"YU, WE HAVE to get out of here. Once they put us in a camp, we have no chance. We won't be able to escape. Just look at my face. This is only a small fraction of what will happen inside a camp. If we leave now, we could leave the country," I quietly plead.

His hollow eyes continue staring at the ground.

"Yu? Please?"

He tears his eyes off the floor and looks straight into my eyes.

"It's hopeless," he mutters.

Hopeless.

Hopeless.

Hopeless.

The word rings in my head.

And I see myself

F

A

L

L

I

N

G

into a dark pit of pain, suffering, and torture.

I see myself screaming,

pleading,

crying.

I see Hala, all alone, painted in red, purple and blue strokes.

I see the inevitable, horrific future we are doing *nothing* to avoid.

Desperation attacks my heart. “We can’t just accept this persecution. We can’t just let them torture us when we’ve done nothing to deserve it. There is hope if we try. Please, Yu...*please.”*

A glimpse of light reflects in his eyes.

"We can run when they open the doors to let some air in.”

“Okay. If you think it’s going to work.” Yu sadly smiles.

Screech.

Thud. Thud.

“Ready, set, *go.*”

Creeeak.

"Woa-"

As soon as the doors open, we run.

“Zuìfàn! Get back here.”

And run.

“They went into the woods.”

And run.

“Search for them everywhere.”

Until the angry footsteps behind us fade into silence.

A cold,

Echoing,

Unsettling silence.

“What if...what if they come back to search for us? What if they’re silently watching us?”

“Shhhh, Yu. You’re making me nervous. Calm down.”

“But what if they do? If they catch us, they might even *kill* us. Shouldn’t we hide somewhere for a while?”

“Where? Tell me, *where?*” I whisper-yell.

Panic ripples through my cold body.

"Please stop yelling. *Please*. What if they hear you?"

Another set of voices echoes through the still air.

"You hear that? They went right. *I told you,"* the "superior" soldier shouts, steel and fire echoing in his voice.

Hide.

Hide.

Hide.

"Ürkesh, up there."

Yu grips onto a quivering branch, reaching higher and higher. I follow, mimicking him until the weaving branches block all the warm, white light. I hug the cracked bark, a tingling gnawing chewing my heart as the *thuds* creep closer,

And closer,

And closer.

"Kill them if you have to. Those dogs don't deserve to live."

"No," the commander shouts, "Don't hurt them. We need them alive. Those are the orders from the government. You can't disobey their commands. You will be punished otherwise."

"I'm tired of your cowardice," the "superior" snaps, his eyes shooting daggers at the commander, "Murder them when you find them."

"You are not this group's leader. Now, obey my orders or else I will report you."

The man's eyes glow red and his teeth shine like the last shine of a knife before it slashes. He runs off, the smoke coming from his ears slowly fading.

"Kai," Yu mutters.

I look at Yu gazing down and lock eyes with the commander. I stumble backward, camouflaging in the shadows.

No. No. Nononono.

He's spotted us.

"The weather is fairly gloomy today. No one should be outside in this weather."

He tears his eyes away and continues on as if he never saw anything.

"Did he just-"

"I don't know, Yu. I don't know."

THUMP. THUMP. THUMP.

Creatures scurry around and birds emerge from their nests, bathing in what little sun is left. My ears ring,

Tick.

Tock.

Tick.

Tock.

Each sound causes my heart to flutter. Time nibbles at me.

Seconds drag on like minutes.

Minutes drag on like hours.

"I think we've waited long enough," I mutter, "Let's go down."

"But Kai-"

"Yu, how long are we going to wait here? They could be miles away. This is our chance. We can't wait here forever. We have to make it as far as possible before dark."

"Shouldn't we wait a little longer? We can even sleep up here, just in case."

"You can wait. I'm going. I can't wait any longer. It's been too long."

"What if they're still here? What if we get caught? Kai, *please* don't."

"We have to go now before it gets dark. We don't have much time left. I'm leaving."

My hand grips each branch, lowering myself down. The creatures rush away and the wind howls as if pushing me. The birds retreat into their nests.

"See, Yu, it's perfectly safe."

I gaze up, only to find a bleached Yu. His eyes look like hollow balls and his mouth is slightly ajar.

THUMP. THUMP.

I scan around until the fiery eyes of a monster meet mine.

7

YETTE

"LET'S GO, you little devil."

Iron hands seize my wrists and drag me through the dirt-speckled snow.

I punch.
I kick.
I fight.
I hurl all my anger at them,
I throw all my anguish at them,
I throw all my frustration at them,
Until they finally

Let

Me

Go.

"Kai."

A dark shape dives and lifts me off the ground.

“Run! Run! Run!”

Click. Click.

Loaded guns surround us, smiling into our faces. We freeze like the snow around us.

"Don't fire," the commander barks. *"Lower your weapons."*

The black rifles drop to the ground, all but one. The "superior's" gun is still aimed at our faces.

"You should let them fire. These are criminals. They tried to escape arrest. They don't deserve to live. They're going to die soon anyway," he yells.

"Put your gun down. You are *not* in charge," the commander warns.

"You don't deserve to lead us with all your sympathy towards these traitors. You *knew* they were up there, didn't you?"

"How dare you accuse an officer of treason and harboring illegal feelings?"

"Do I have to remind you of the boy you tried to so bravely save?"

"I have said this once and I will repeat it. *I am the commander*. You are *not*. Lower your voice and learn to respect those in authority, or there will be consequences."

"I don't care whether you are commander or not. I'm tired of listening to you. *I am taking control of this group like I deserve to."*

His finger rests on the trigger.

"Yu, get down!"

I shove Yu to the dirt and pin him down.

Tetetetete.

Bullets rip through the trees as the "superior" blindly shoots. The commander lunges at him and the gun flies out of his hand. The commander's pistol glares at the traitor's face.

"Arrest him," he orders coldly.

The soldiers drag him into another police truck, one with windows and leather seats while we're led to a windowless prison.

The commander nods to the rest of the guards.

I'm sorry, he mouths, a silent tear dripping down his cheek. The van swallows us.

D a r k n e s s

SCREEEEECH.

The exhausted car pants to a stop and collapses. It opens up to let the cool, heavy air fill it up and throw its prisoners out.

Outside, the joyous sun beams, scattering its warm light onto the sky. Threads of white glide in and out, weaving themselves into the delicate, blue blanket.

But that light refuses to look at the camp.

All the horrors and nightmares that rage on inside stream out, clouding it in a gloomy storm. Gray and black fly around it, singing

This

Is

Your

Home.

"Move."

Thunder booms in my head as day vanishes and I enter a

Cold,

Everlasting night.

A million things hit me at once as each of my senses explodes. It's like someone threw rotten eggs, reeking socks and sweat together. Bruises and cuts paint everyone's bodies and the hope and warmth are sucked out of their eyes to leave empty glass balls. Invisible chains lash out and tangle our wrists, tying us to the camp. Rabid wolves circle their hideout in search of prey.

You are stuck here forever, Ürkesh...

The camp becomes a harsh voice whispering in my mind.

Let me go. Please.

Do you really think I will? I never let my prey go. Never. Even if you try to flee, you won't make it. I have an electric, barbed wire fence to ensure you stay, and I have cameras watching every step.

"Move," the soldier barks again, the butt of his rifle shoving us into the camp.

Sights, smells, and sounds bombard me like a catapult as a shadowy building covers the horizon, blocking the sun but allowing the clouds in. The stony dirt scratches against our feet. The coppery blood lingers in my mouth and my watermelon-sized cheek protrudes as if someone stuffed a basketball in it. Empty, blue suits wander around the facility, the invisible faces cast down in humiliation. Their arms are exposed with numbers branded onto their skin. Even animals are given names but we are just given numbers. We're only worth a bunch of numbers.

The distant moon is just like Hala, beautiful but so far away. The wind whistles, carrying ash-like particles that form a figure. A figure I know. Hala, but young like she was when we used to wrestle. She always used to win until last year, when I won for the first time. A brick lodges in my throat. I boasted so much. She tried again and again as my taunting grew harsher and harsher until she gave up. Until she gave up everything. That's when she withdrew into herself and isolated herself from the world. She tried to become her normal self but her brother didn't let her. That's when she was taken captive and her parents were taken. She was taken captive when her brother gave up. She was taken captive when her brother didn't fight hard enough. She was taken captive when her brother abandoned her.

She's gone because of *me.*

I didn't fight hard enough.

I didn't protect her.

I let her down.

I gave up.

"GET UP," a guard barks.

We fly out of the cell, silent squeals escaping at the sight of iron whips. The line leads to the other side of the camp, where labor or torture awaits. Human-like robots march to their designated places. The beast inside threatens to free itself as I try to keep it quiet.

Wrrrrrm. Wrrrrrm.

It keeps on growing and roaring, summoning the thunder to take its place. Lightning flashes inside and burns the metal walls as a fire runs and runs until it can't be extinguished any longer. The storm clouds my head and balls of blue run away from the menacing footsteps as they inch closer and closer. My legs slush as water seeps out from the storm. I collapse onto the floor, clutching my stomach.

"Hey, what are you doing?"

The blob smashes a rock at my head. A wet stream drips down my face. The storm only grows angrier and angrier at the aggravation. The lightning continues tearing and the fire continues licking all it can. It spreads, my whole body in white-hot pain. Bile climbs up my throat, threatening to spill out of my mouth.

"Get up."

The blurs turn into crisp images as the storm backs away from the command.

"What is *wrong* with you? Are you deaf? Time to work, not lay on the floor. You've already slept enough."

"I...I'm so sorry, sir."

"That doesn't answer my question."

"I was hungry, sir. I haven't eaten in two days. I'm sorry."

"What is your name, *Móguǐ?"*

A knife jams into my heart.

"Kai, sir."

"So you're a new one, eh? I haven't heard of you yet. Boys, here's one who needs a lesson. He hasn't been taught the proper rules of humanity yet. *Aw*, you want your mama, little boy? Where could she be? Boys, do you know where she is? Hurry and get her here before her child throws a tantrum."

Thump.

"Look, the little boy is about to cry."

Thump.

"He's scared. We need to find his mama before he starts to cry or we'll have a big mess on our hands."

Thump. Thump.

"What's your mama's name, boy?"

Thumpthump.

"He's a quiet one, we need to make him talk. Do you want a toy, baby? Or a piece of candy?"

THUMPTHUMPTHUMP.

Smack. Crash.

"Who's your God, *gǒu?"*

Blank.

"Answer me."

"A...A...Allah."

Crack. Smash.

The wind morphs into a familiar face.

"Hala, what are you doing here?"

"The real question is, what are you doing?"

"I'm trying to survive."

"Are you sure?"

"I don't have any other choice."

"You do. You always have the option to fight back. Fight them. Show them that you're not the animal they think you are. Don't give in."

"What about you?"

"I am fighting, just not in front of you. You could have seen me if..."

"If what?"

"If you would have...fought...harder."

Fought harder.

Fought harder.

If I had fought harder.

A glass mirror shatters, all of its millions of pieces on the floor, crying. A blue fire rages inside, eating slowly.

"So...so this is all my fault?"

She looks straight into my eyes, searching. A red fire dances inside her eyes.

"Yes, this is *all* your fault. You could have fought harder so we wouldn't be in a concentration camp. You could have fought harder so *I* wouldn't be suffering in this torture chamber *alone*. So that we could have fought together. You could have fought harder so we would have escaped this bitter country but *no*. You had to be that coward you always were. You had to be selfish and save yourself. Of course, you are with your best friend, Yu, right? You wouldn't dare leave his side, even if that meant leaving mine. Do you know how much I've suffered because of *you?* I've only had myself for over three years. You never paid attention to me. I was just...a thorn in your side. Something that you needed to get rid of."

"Hala, I'm sorry. I'm really sorry."

"As if sorry is enough to get us out of here. As if sorry is going to bring Mama and Papa back. As if sorry is going to let us find each other."

Woooooooo.

The breeze starts.

"Hala, come back. *Wait for me*."

"You couldn't wait for me, so now, I can't wait for you."

Hala melts into ashes and the breeze carries them far away, to the blissful garden where tears don't exist.

"*Hala, please. Please wait. Please, wait.*" A lone tear streams down my face.

Crack.

Aaaaah.

"That's enough. If I ever catch you goofing around again, you will get more than this."

All I can see is the whip in his hand. Everything else fades into nothing. The whip continues cackling.

And cackling.

And cackling.

"Get up."

I try. I try but my legs collapse underneath me as if a wave pushed down an old man.

"Get up."

Crack.

The whip screams in my face as it slaps me right on my cheek and it swells like someone stuffed a basketball in it. I can feel the red. I can feel the blood oozing out. I can feel the fire eating my face. My face tingles and tears well in my eyes.

I stagger forward, white-hot pain searing through my whole body. Daggers lodge into my back as the pain pulls me up like strings attached to a puppet. But the strings are only so strong.

Snap.

They crack and tear until the puppet sinks onto another nearby screaming puppet.

THUMPTHUMP.

"Kai."

THUMP THUMP.

"Kai."

Thump Thump.

"Kai."

Thump.

"*Kai.*"

Thu-

"*Kai!*"

8

SEKKIZ

UHHHHHHU.

"Kai, it's okay. You're okay... It was just a dream."

What happened? Where am I? Why is it so dark? Why is it so quiet?

"Kai? Kai?"

"Huh?"

"Kai, can't you hear me?"

"What is this place? Who are you?"

"This isn't the time to joke around," the figure mutters.

"Yu? Is that you? Where am I?"

"Don't you remember?"

"No."

"You don't remember...anything?"

"The last thing I remember is that old lady giving us that delicious soup."

The broken look on his face is all I need to know there is a lot more to the story.

"Yu, what happened? What's going on? Where are we?"

"The police came."

"Where's Hala...Where's Hala...Yu, where is Hala? *Answer me*."

"She's somewhere else."

"Where?"

"A different camp."

"How? How? How? How? *How, Yu*?"

"They took her, Kai. They took her. Anger can't solve anything. Calm down. *Please.* Panicking will only make everything worse."

"How?"

"Stop now, Kai. Please don't cry. We'll find a way out of here. We'll find her."

We, not you. We're in this together.

"Thank you."

"Back to work," a deep voice bellows.

"Come on."

The second my feet touch the stone floor, a towering cobra jerks and strikes, leaving red gashes in its wake. The searing, hot pain stings like electricity. I wobble around like a fish out of water, gasping its last, deep breaths.

"Kai, what's wrong?"

"Nothing. My back hurts. It's really nothing."

"Nothing? You just don't remember..."

"Don't remember what?"

Silence.

"Yu, what do I not remember? What do I not remember? Tell me. Tell me right *now,* Yu."

"Shhh. Please stop yelling at me. The guards will hear you. They...they whipped you."

"But...whips don't exist. Guns do but whips don't."

"Anything is possible here, Kai. They have everything. All the horrifying torture devices you can ever think of. Everything that has existed, exists and will exist. *Everything*. Nothing *doesn't* exist here."

"Are you coming or what? How long does it take to get off the floor?" the guard growls, his rifle poking through the door. His shadow swells as his eyes peep through.

"Hurry, Kai. Before he comes here himself and gives us double of what you got. *Hurry up."*

"I'm trying, Yu. It takes a while to stand after you're whipped."

With my arm draped around his neck, I limp into a smokey room.

It's as if a colony of ants wiggles in the factory. The room is full of breathing machines and workers swarm around the sides. After the white fluffs go through the stomach of the machine, they're spit out as balls of thread, tended to by millions of workers. Boxes are scattered on the floor and there isn't an inch of space that doesn't have a crate. Young, old, tall, short, weak, strong, all scramble to fill every box until it is full.

"Hey, what do you think you're doing?"

A huge ball-like object buries into my side.

"You snake. This is for the *adults.* You're a *child.* You go there," he points to a rusty, wrinkled door.

"Ye...yes, sir."

My feet turn into little bodies and control themselves, leading me to the door. It screams and coughs as the rushing light fills the emptiness of the building. The sun laughs outside as the white smiles. Rustling sprouts topped with white clouds cover the horizon. The numbing breeze chills my bones and my teeth clatter together. It's as if I'm looking into a picture.

"Fill this up."

A boom disrupts that dream. My heart drops back down to Earth. Even in the most beautiful of places, there is always darkness. There is always rotten in every barrel of ripe, crispy apples. There is always injustice *somewhere,* even if there is justice everywhere else.

I tear at the white fluffs as the guard's eyes shoot daggers at me. The amber-like residue clings to my fingers and some cotton sticks and soon, my hands look like clouds.

I look up and swipe my hair away when movement catches my eye. A tall man appears from a shack and a guard trails closely behind him, whispering something. The man nods, shoos the guard away and remains there, surveying the area until his eyes land on me.

"Is that man looking at *me?"* I ask Yu.

Yu turns around and sneaks a look at him.

"I think so and it's getting creepy. Let's move somewhere else."

We swim through the cotton plants until we reach an empty area.

"Yu?"

"Yes?"

"What do you think happened to our parents?"

Yu's eyes hollow and I'm left looking into the eyes of a dead boy.

"I'm sorry. I didn't mean it that way. I...I forgot."

"No, no, it's fine. Promise me you won't leave, Kai. You're the only person I have left."

"You know I won't. Why are you crying? Please don't cry, Yu. Please don't."

"They killed my parents. They murdered them."

"At least you managed to get away. There was nothing you could've done to save them."

"I didn't escape." His eyes bulge out once realizing what he had said. A shadow blankets his already hollow eyes.

"What do you mean? How did you *not* escape? You told me you did. You would have been dead otherwise."

"I...I...I.."

"You what? Tell me what's wrong, Yu. Come on."

"I told them something they wanted to hear."

"And what was that? Yu, what was it?"

My heart bangs against my chest like a gong, each *thump* sending panic throughout me. A boulder lodges in my throat and the air sprints out of my lungs. The blood pounds against my head. A Chinese soldier will *never, ever* let a Uyghur go free. Never.

"Itoldthemwhereyouwerehiding."

Electricity shoots through my brain and my mind explodes until I can't feel anything anymore. My legs turn into waves and my heart rips my chest open. A surge of boiling blood *thumps* in my head and I turn crimson.

I can't control the anger.
The loss.
The betrayal.

Thump thump.
Thumpthump.
THUMPTHUMP.
THUMPTHUMPTHUMP.
"You. Did. What? You. Told. Them. What?"

"I'm sorry. They *made* me. They would have done the same to me otherwise."

"My parents are dead because of *you*. Hala is gone because of *you*. You're a traitor. And you pretend as if you're my *friend*. Do you hear that? A *traitor*. You're a lying snake. A black crow. You're worse than the government itself. "

Yu breaks into a million glass pieces, each one sobbing as the ground drinks the tears. He sprints as far as possible, the wind fighting and trying to restrain him. The clouds turn dark and block the sunlight.

He deserved that. He deserves to be killed. He deserves every single punishment the camp supervisor can ever think of.

He killed my parents.

He killed Hala.

They're gone because of him.

The fire transforms into water, escaping uncontrollably from my eyes.

“Why are you crying?” a squeaky, hushed voice calls from underneath me. I look down at a little girl clinging to my legs.

"Me hongry. Me hongry."

It’s as if her tiny hand is tugging at my heart. A cold feeling travels through my blood and the tears stop dripping.

I wish I would have been thankful for the vegetables I had to eat before all this.

I snatch the minuscule piece of blue, rock-like bread from my pocket and hand it to the girl. She looks at it, then at me. She looks at it again and back at me.

"You can have it."

She glares at the bread and within a flash, gobbles it up, a toothless smile spreading on her grape-like face. I wait, and wait, and wait for her to get off my legs but she doesn't. She continues clinging to me like a monkey hanging onto its mom as I shove more fluffs down the bag. Sometimes, she glances back, as if looking for someone until the darkness sets in and the blanket of sleep wraps around me.

9

TOQQUZ

"ATTENTION. Everyone must report to the facility's entrance immediately."

A storm of people floods out of the fields and I'm swept into a barren, open area.

A towering, statue-like man climbs a pedestal and his eyes shoot daggers into each one of ours. It's as if he emerged from a painting we studied in art. He looks like he could be Xi Jinping's son. A prominent, neat bush sprouts on his head and a pistol rests in his belt. A bright fire rages inside his dark eyes and the smoke streams out of his nose. He's an image of a living, breathing dragon, the hatred, cruelty and ruthlessness combined into one body.

He's the man who was watching me.

"There have been rumors of a resident running away. It is of the most importance to find who it is. Roll call will begin. Number one."

"Here."

"Number two."

"Here."

He reads like he's reading an everlasting poem. My mind wanders to the edge of time. It sits there, observing the environment until an echoing explosion of a booming voice whizzes me back to reality.

"Where is he? Number 108? Yu? Yu? He's the criminal who escaped. Do not worry. This will be taken very seriously. Take that boy and question him. The two were close."

"What?" The words slip out but fall on closed ears. Arms swarm over me like a colossal wave, thrashing objects around until they settle down. The subtle chirps of doors and the scurried *thuds* of feet are all that buzz around me. They're like bees, the *bzzzzzzz* drilling into your head until a deep, permanent hole stays there. Blurs of black fade and reappear as the blue of the sky, the yellow of the sun and the white of the clouds blur until only the darkness is left.

"Now, child. I'm Chen, the supervisor of this camp. I ask only one thing of you during this interview. It is one of the most basic values each human being must possess. Do you know the answer?"

"N...no, sir," I stutter, trying to swallow my fear.

"It seems your mother didn't teach you the basics of living like a human. Proof of your barbaric lifestyle. What a shame. If only you were educated," he sighs. "The answer is honesty. You must tell the truth. Lying only takes you to *hell.* Being honest, no matter how hard, is always the right thing. That's what your religion teaches, right?"

I can't help but nod. This man acts as if he *is* the president's son or even the president himself.

"Good. This is the relationship I look for. One where we understand each other. We're quite similar, you and me. I can feel it. It's as if you're a *part* of me. Now, do you know a boy named Yu?"

"Y...yes."

"Were you two friends?"

"We *were."*

"You still are but you don't admit it. Yu is your best friend," a misty voice surfaces.

Who is that? I peer around. It's only Chen and me and that wasn't Chen. It must have been my imagination.

"Boy? Boy? Hello?"

"Huh? Oh. I'm so sorry, sir. I...I zoned out."

"You *zoned out* while your superior is talking? What kind of disrespect is this? *Tsk. Tsk.* These are basic manners. Your mother hasn't taught you anything, has she," he clicks his tongue as if he's a disappointed dad whose son broke the window.

"I'm sorry, sir."

"I'll let this go but only because I like you. You seem like a boy who could rise to become part of the human race. Now, where were we? Oh, yes. Did Yu ever talk about running away?"

The question hits like a gong. Yu was talking about escaping the second we got here but I can't tell Chen that. But Yu *did* betray me.

"No, sir," I force out, controlling the urge to say yes.

"What did you two talk about?"

"Random stuff."

"What random stuff?"

"About how great work is and how deluded our...parents were. How the Han Chinese saved us from our innate inclination towards evil. How the government provided us with opportunities to grow and rise to be of the best race and how in the end, we will grow to repay them," I read off the textbook I was forced to read in school.

"Interesting. Guards? Take him outside. You should never have lied, *Xíngshì*. I'm an *officer*. I know how you prisoners are. You think you're smarter than those in authority. This "cleverness" will cost you your *life* one day."

"I'm telling the truth."

"That's exactly what a liar would say. Take him away."

"No. Wait. *I'm telling the truth*."

"You dare raise your voice in front of your supervisor? I forgave you once but I won't again. You've had too many chances. You are taking advantage of my kindness. Guards. Take him."

"Please. Please. Please."

My body scrapes and scratches the ground as two ruthless bulls drag me to an inescapable reality. My heart beats, screaming,

You're going to die.

You're going to die.

You're going to die.

A looming, threatening building traps the sun behind it and cackles as a new meal arrives at its mouth. It drinks all of my energy until only a sack of skin is left.

I let them tie me up.

I let them start the machine.

I let them do whatever they want.

Glunk.

I try freeing my hands but it's no use against metal. The air narrowly escapes the closing prison of my throat as water surges inside. My eyes burn like they have been thrown into a fire and my lungs collapse.

The water breaks open and the air suddenly floods into my chest but only for a few seconds before the water is everywhere again.

"Are you willing to stop lying?" Chen asks.

"Mhm. Mhm. Mhm."

The board emerges as the intense, fiery eyes of the guards bore into me.

"I don't know why he escaped. I don't know where he is. I didn't even know he escaped until the announcement. If I knew anything, I would have told you. I would have told you before you would have called me. Please, let me go. *Please*. I swear I'm telling the truth."

"Do you think I believe your oaths? You're a stinking liar, like the rest of your kind."

Clink.

I grasp as much air as possible before I'm shoved into the water again. I try not to let the burning air out of my lungs but weakness overcomes me. Flashes of black dance before my eyes and my mouth can't hold the air trying to free itself from me. It floats away in giant bubbles, celebrating its freedom but leaving me to die. That's when a dark figure wraps me in its cold blanket, putting me into a deep, deep sleep.

10

ON

"HALA. MAMA. PAPA."

There they are. Blobs of light embracing each other. Their smiles light the Earth and stretch across the horizon. Papa's joy radiates like the sun, warming each and every object for miles. Mama's happiness glistens like the moon, guiding creatures in the pitch black. Hala smiles like the stars, twinkling in a rhythm. Their arms are all wrapped around each other.

Their light crashes into me like a wave as my entire body surges with unfound energy. I dash towards them but each step makes them a mile farther until I freeze. Something hot and sticky pulls me to the ground.

I struggle to free my legs but each tug makes them sink deeper.

I look down to find myself sinking in a lake

Of

Blood.

"Let me go."

"No. You can't. You can't go to them."

"I have to. They're my family. I belong with them."

"It will only make things way worse. You won't understand. Please. Listen. Don't go to them or else...You will never get out of here," a sharp voice cackles.

Chen.

"Please. Let me go."

"You don't deserve to go with them. It will only make everything so, so much worse. I have the power to kill them all."

I lurch out, clawing at the grass until I shoot out like a cannonball. Instantly on my feet, I run

And run

And run

Towards them.

Towards my family.

But the instant my hand reaches out to grip Mama's hand, to scratch Papa's beard, to hug Hala, they fade like ghosts. Blood replaces them. It flows down my hands and clings on like rope.

Drip. Drip.

Desperation soars into my neck, fighting to escape only to give up. That's when it finds a better way. It attacks my heart.

Aaaaaah.

Crack.

"Shut up, *Gǒu*. You're not a baby. Don't tell me you miss your mama already," Chen laughs deeply while the others join, exploding like bombs around me. "I'll ask you *one more time.* Where. Is. Yu?"

"I don't know, sir. He loved you. He idolized you. I don't understand why he left or where he went. If I did, I would have told you. Lying is a sin. I would never lie to you."

Chen glares into my eyes as if reading my mind. Knives shoot out of them and glide right through my eyes as the air grows hard and still.

"Let him go."

Clink. Clank.

The chains drop to the floor as the guard unfastens all the locks tangling my body.

"You must collect double the amount of cotton due to what happened yesterday. After all, we need productive workers, or we have no use for you slaves."

"Y...yes, sir," I stammer, glad to be out of Chen's grip.

WHOOOOOOSSH.

A gust of wind strokes my face and a bushful of hair flies by. Curiosity seeps into my heart. What...*Who* was that? I survey the area. No one in sight. My legs move on their own in the direction the figure went. No sign of the person. It must have been my imagination.

I drag myself back to the cotton field when my eyes catch a dark bundle on the grass. Clothes? I peer from side to side, but only the chirping of crickets greets me. Why would someone leave their clothes on the ground?

A lightbulb flashes above my head and I'm whizzed into a distant memory.

"Do you exercise or something?" Yu asks.

"Uhhhhhh....no. Why?"

"How did you get so tall? You're like a foot taller than me and your arms are double my size."

"I don't know. I've never really thought about it. It's natural, I guess."

I throw the uniform over myself. The sleeves droop down and the pants keep on slipping. I pull the metal cap down my face so only my mouth is visible.

My stomach twists, squeezing.

My blood heats up, blazing.

My heart pounds, screaming,

Hurry.

Hurry.

Hurry.

I scan the area and begin to run towards the camp's exit. I try to run far,

far

away.

Away from the pain.

Away from the torture.

"Hey, where do you think you're going?"

No.

No.

No.

I turn around to face a short, stocky man with a gun perched on his shoulder. A group of soldiers stands behind him.

I stick my chest out. "I have to go to the bathroom."

"There are bathrooms inside. Go there."

"I don't want to go where the stinking Uyghurs go."

He scans me for a few seconds.

"For a second, I thought you were a Uyghur but now that I think about it, what kind of Uyghur would disguise himself as a guard? They aren't that smart," the man laughs. "Ah, I'm just messing with you. You're good to go. Besides, it's the perfect excuse to get out of here. It gives you a break from that Chen guy. He's new and acts like he's the ruler of this place. We've been here longer than he has. We deserve to run this place. Who died and made him king? If I were you, I would spend some time in the bathroom."

"Good idea. Now, I have to go before I have an accident," I wink, trying to act normal.

"Have a great time," the man winks back.

Now's your chance. Run.

As soon as he turns around, I rush.

I rush to leave the camp.

I rush to search for my family.

Crash.

I slam right into a large, stone-like object. As the figure clears up, my eyes meet a burning, vicious gaze.

11

ON BIR

"WHERE ARE YOU GOING?"

Chen digs into my eyes, searching.

Thump.

Thump thump.

Thumpthumpthump.

THUMP. THUMP. THUMP.

His stare searches in my eyes and enters my mind, where my plan lays open.

“I was going back to camp, sir.”

Chen sucks at his cigarette.

"Camp is that way," he points in the direction I came from.

"Oh...my apologies, sir. I'm new here and I don't know my way around. I got lost in the woods."

"New, huh? I wasn't informed of a *new* soldier. What's your name and what are you doing out of the facility?"

"My name is Peng, sir, and I was going to the bathroom. I can't tolerate being in the re-education center with those pigs. I had to get out."

"Hmm...I don't remember being told about you. Who sent you?"

"I don't remember his name, but he's a commander."

"Of course a commander sent you. Why would you not remember the name of your leader?"

"No one ever called him by his name. He went as 'commander.'"

"Describe him."

"He is of average height, has blue eyes and has graying hair that reaches his ears. He is pretty thin and looks about ten years younger than he actually is," I rant, describing the commander.

"Ah, I know who you're talking about. Since you are new, you will be under my supervision for a few days. You need to go through *proper training* before becoming a real soldier. You need to prove your utmost loyalty to me and the state. Now, I have a specific task for you to complete. If you complete it well, you will be rewarded. I need a man I can fully trust, especially with those lazy brats acting as 'guards.'"

"I will be that soldier, sir. What do you need?" I force out.

My plan is...falling.

Falling.

Falling

I don't want to do anything to help Chen.

I don't want anything to do with him.

All I want is to leave.

To get back to my family.

"Follow me. *Please."*

As he speeds ahead, I slow down. If he gets far enough, I can run. This is my only chance.

A glimpse of hope floats into my heart. Maybe I actually can run away from this misery.

"Hey, pick up the pace. I don't have the rest of my life to watch you take baby steps to the facility. If you want to stay, prove it to me."

"Yes, sir."

Desperation bubbles inside my chest.

My.

Plan.

Has.

Completely.

Failed.

If Chen discovers what I tried to do, I will never see the light of day again. He *can't* find out.

"What do you want me to do, sir?"

"I need you to deliver this experimental vial to Room 23. You know where it is, right?"

"No, sir."

"Hmh...take the stairs to the basement and turn right. It'll be the first room you see."

"You can count on me, sir."

"Hmm..."

I wander around in my head as I trudge down the stairs. The hallway stinks of mold and beyond each step, everything is shrouded in darkness. Squeaking creatures scurry around, singing their own songs.

A dim glow glistens under a crack. This must be the door.

Creeeeeeeak.

Aaaaaah.

As the door whines open, all that tears my ears are screams.

Blood-curdling,

Pained,

Echoing screams.

They ring in my head, replacing all of my panic with fear. Chills creep up my spine as a sudden realization dawns upon me. I've never actually *seen* anyone being tortured. I've hardly experienced anything.

This is where the real agony begins. This is where the guards become bloodthirsty monsters.

These are the Black Rooms.

"No, no, no, please, please. Pleasepleaseplease. I'll do anything. *Please.*"

"No. *Shut. Up.* You thugs don't know how to respect those superior to you. You can only be taught with the whip."

The woman continues begging, pleading, as if the words went right through her head, having no impact.

Crack. Crack.

"Even the whip doesn't teach you manners. There is only one more way left and believe me, it is the *worst."*

"No. No. Please. Ple-"

Slush.

Horror seizes my heart and it pounds, screaming to be let out. A hand grips my heart, choking it. A hammer strikes my head as the air grows hot and metallic, struggling to go down my throat. A blizzard ensues in my spine and the ice creeps through my veins. The air rustles, singing,

Slush.

Slush.

Slush.

"You dogs are useless. You all deserve to be killed. You were made for that very reason."

The man continues slashing as I dare myself to peer into the room. A crazed animal grips the bayonet and drives it through the woman's body, again and again and again. He looks like the devil, red horns sticking out of his head. He glares hungrily at the pool of blood. The red bayonet in his hands begins to drip and the body looks like an eaten animal corpse. It's all a lump of crimson flesh.

"What are you looking at?"

"Nothing, sir."

"You'd better be. Now move along."

My eyes catch the sign in the door and all the color on my face drains and I turn into ice. *This* is Room 23.

12

ON IKKI

"WHY ARE YOU still standing there? *Move."*

"Chen sent me here, sir. He said to give you this vial," I stammer, the yellowish liquid dancing in the bottle.

He suddenly transforms from an animal to a gentleman, the fire still dancing in his eyes. "Ah, thank you," He snatches the vial. "Do you want to know what this is?"

"N...No, sir."

"It's acid."

"A...a...acid?"

"Yep."

"What do you plan on doing with the...acid?"

"What do you think? Of course, I will use it on one of these dogs. The question is, who to use it on?"

"H...H...."

"Say it, boy. Stop stuttering before I use it on you."

"Ho...How about you use the acid on her?"

Please say yes. Please say yes.

"Nah, she's dead. It'll be no use on a dead woman. I need a *new* test subject," he smiles hungrily.

I have to get that bottle before he uses it on someone. A blizzard travels down my spine. The thought of him throwing acid on someone's face makes me feel like -1576 degrees.

"I need a favor. You think you're up for the job?"

"Yes, sir."

"I need you to find me a *specimen* to test this acid on."

"Specimen? Wha...What do you mean?"

"You know what I mean. Now, go before I *make* you."

"Yes, sir."

As my rushed footsteps slam against the floor, questions race through my mind.

Why? Why do that to a human? Who will it be? How will I stop him? How will I ever escape from this place?

Thud.

My feet clamor up the steps.

Creak.

The door screams.

Aaaah.

My mind yells in panic as it races to realize the depth of my situation and rushes to find a solution.

I could kill the soldier. I could...use the acid on him. I could pretend to throw it on a person but miss.

My mind explodes as lightning cracks inside. Thunder booms, rupturing my ears. Everything transforms into blurs and tears pour out, like a shower of rain.

"Ürkesh, take a deep breath. Calm down. Clear your mind. To see, you need to forget everything. You need a calm, empty mind to think. You have to work the problem through. Panicking will make everything worse and then, you will get caught. That could mean losing your and Hala's lives."

My head perks up at the sound of a deep, soothing, gentle voice.

"Who's there?" I peep.

"I'm you."

How?

"I'm your inner voice. I'm here to help you but only if you take a few deep breaths. Now, do you feel better?"

Yes.

"Now, stop and think. How to prevent the soldier from doing what he wants to do?"

By not letting him.

"And how to do that?"

Well, I could pretend not to find anyone suitable.

"And?" he asks with such curiosity, it is impossible to resist answering.

He will be forced to look for someone and that will give me time to get rid of the flask.

"Wouldn't it be suspicious if you get rid of the bottle?"

Hmm...yeah. It would be. I could replace the acid with a harmless substance and that will force him to deal with the fact that the acid is not effective. That could lead to the entire supply of acid going to waste.

"There you go. See what happens when you slow down and think? A free mind is an effective one. Now, calmly enact your plan."

"Sir-"

"Did you find what I asked for?"

"No."

"What they say is true. In the end, you have to do everything yourself. You're a useless piece of junk like the barbarians imprisoned here. Now, stay here while I go do *your* work."

My mouth clamps shut. Fear knots in my throat and my heart *thumps* like crazy. That's when a glimmer temporarily blinds my eyes. The vial. It's still in his belt. If I don't get it, my whole plan goes to waste. Everything will go to waste.

"Grab it," The Voice chirps.

How?

"Like pickpockets stealing wallets."

"It only took five minutes. Five minutes to find someone suitable and you couldn't even do that much. *You couldn't even spend five minutes.* All you had to do was grab the nearest, healthiest person you could find and drag them here. How hard is that? You are testing my patience."

The officer storms into the room with a bruised child stumbling behind him.

"I'm sorry, sir."

"Don't call me 'sir.' Call me Officer Feng."

"Yes, Officer Feng."

"Now, be of some use and hold this boy down." Feng tosses the toddler like a rock and he falls into my arms. His eyes are painted red and purple-bluish patches are blotted all over him. The boy's skin is like a desert, barren, dry and cracked while his hair is torn in patches. His eyes are painted red and purple-bluish patches are blotted all over him. His hollow eyes beg and plead for help. They light a cool fire inside me and it chews at my heart.

"Now, where did that vial go?"

Clink.

A gust of air escapes my lungs as his foot brushes against the bottle.

"Huh, I don't remember it being colorless," Feng mumbles.

Please fall for it. Please fall for it.

"Hold him still and make sure you're not in the way unless you want to be permanently deformed."

I pin the boy down as his eyes plead. The tape on his mouth crinkles and folds as he tries to say something. The chains jingle as they rub against each other but to no avail. All the silent begging falls on hard hearts, blind eyes and shut ears. Fat tears drip down his face.

I place my index finger on my lips and squeeze his hand.

Don't worry, I mouth.

You will be okay. He can't hurt you with his acid, no matter how hard he tries.

Swish.

Silence.

No fizzling.

No bubbling.

No screaming.

Just silence.

Deafening, piercing silence.

The boy's closed eyes open up.

"Why didn't it work? I knew it. I knew it wouldn't work. It's junk, just like you."

Crash.

The boy crumples from Feng's kick. The man turns into a hyena, tearing and clawing at its prey. He punches, kicks, scratches, and bites the toddler until blood pools on the ground like an endless sea of red, his still body barely floating. Blood sprays out of the child's mouth and Feng pants, his eyes still burning.

"Feng, stop. Put the boy down."

Chen.

Chen's here.

He'll see right through this. He'll know everything.

"Feng, did you hear me?"

"Yes, sir."

"Why didn't you listen?"

"I'm sorry, sir."

"Make sure this *never* happens again. Don't let your rage control you. This is your last chance. Next time, I will have you fired and the government will decide what to do with you."

"Ye...Yes, sir," Feng stutters.

Chen turns towards me. "You are dismissed."

I nod, fixing my eyes on the ground as the stone tiles blur.

Crack.

A hand clamps to my neck like the talons of an eagle. My throat struggles to remain open as the force squeezes. The air claws its way in and out of my throat and my heart screams.

THUMP. THUMP. THUMP.

"Not. So. Fast."

13

ON ÜCH

"I'M AWARE OF all activities in this camp, so no matter what you do, I will always know. *Always*. Do you understand?"

"Yes, sir," I croak, the words barely rolling off my tongue.

"*I* was the one to put that uniform outside. I knew it was you when I stopped you on the road. *I* was the one to tell those soldiers to let you pass through. And why, you might ask? Because I wanted to see you suffer. I wanted to see you panic and lose control. But that doesn't mean this will go unpunished. You shouldn't have been so gullible. You should have known that acting smart will result in huge consequences. You will *never* get out of this place alive, ever, no matter how hard you try. *Guards. Take him."*

The words are trapped in my throat.

My body is stuck.

My limbs are frozen.

There is no escape.

The only way is to survive.

The realization echoes like a gong. This is a concentration camp. I can't escape. There are hundreds of armed men and women and I haven't thought of the possibility of cameras. On top of that, the clever monster, Chen, knows everything that occurs in this camp. He knows this place inside out. After all, it is his facility.

The dust soars as my legs scrape the ground. The chains binding my wrists and ankles rattle like bells singing a merry song, having no idea how cruel reality is. They sing as if this is a pleasant dream while the pleading screams resonate throughout the building.

Thwack.

The soldiers throw me inside the cell like a ball tossed into a closet. All the energy has drained out of me. I'm so tired; everything feels like a dream. Two glowing eyes stare out from the darkness. Now, I'm definitely dreaming.

"Kai?"

I'm *definitely* dreaming.

"Kai? Is that really you? Kai. Kai. *Kai."*

Sturdy, stick arms shake me until my brain is wobbling.

"Yu? Yu. Yu."

"Kai."

The tears pour out like a raging waterfall.

"I...I'm...so...so...sorry. I didn't mean any of it. I shouldn't have gotten mad. I shouldn't have yelled at you. I'm so sorry."

"No, I'm sorry. You were right to be upset at me. It was justified. I shouldn't have told the soldiers. I shouldn't have betrayed you."

"No, it wasn't. I shouldn't have yelled at you. I shouldn't have been upset. I shouldn't have said what I said. You did what you had to. You had to tell them to survive. At least you're alive. That's what matters. I still can't believe you're okay."

"They caught me. All the effort I put into escaping is down the drain. Now, I'm going to die here."

"They caught me too but it's okay. At least we'll die together. Then, we will be out of this place. We will be reunited with our families and live forever in everlasting bliss."

"Enough chit-chat. This isn't a hotel."

Chen.

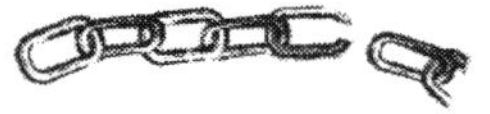

"MARCH ON! Heroes of every race!

The great Communist Party leads us in continuing the Long March!

Millions with but one heart toward a communist tomorrow

Bravely struggle to develop and protect the motherland.

March on! March on, March on!

We will for many generations

Raise high Mao Zedong's banner! March on!

Raise high Mao Zedong's banner! March on!

March on! March on! On!"

"Continue!" Chen barks.

"There is no new China without the Communist Party.

There is no new China without the Communist Party.

The Communist Party toil for the nation.

His the Communist Party of one mind saved China.

He pointed to the road of the liberation of the people.

He led China towards the light.

He insisted the war for more than eight years.

He improved people's lives.

He built a base behind enemy lines.

He carries many benefits of democracy.

It practiced democracy, bringing many advantages.

Without the Communist Party, there would be no new China.

Without the Communist Party, there would be no new China."

"Continue."

"No one deserves our love more
Than the ones who have saved us
From imminent danger and destruction
No one deserves more praise
Than the ones who spread peace
And justice throughout the land
No one deserves this
Except for Xi Jinping."

That was the last paper to read...unless Chen brings more. How do people come up with these poems? They're terrible. They don't even rhyme. Whoever wrote them is a *terrible* poet and the one making us read them is worse.

"Now, here are five sheets of paper each. Your *assignment* is to write a reflective essay on how evil the souls of Uyghurs are. You must fill each and every page with words. If there is a single wasted space, you will be punished. Understand?"

"Yes, sir." Yu and I mumble.

"What was that?"

"Yes, sir."

"Louder."

"Yes, sir."

"I...have a question."

"Go ahead, dumb little boy."

"Are we supposed to write on both sides of each paper?"

"What a brilliant question. Maybe you all aren't as dumb as I think you are. Did you all hear what he asked?"

"No," a chorus responds.

"He asked if they're supposed to use both sides of the paper. What a smart boy! What do you all think the answer is?"

"Yes," the chorus booms.

Chen smirks at us. *"Kai,"* Yu chastises.

"Sorry."

But we both know the reality. Chen would have punished us more if we hadn't written on both sides. It's better to ask than to regret it later on. It's better to break our arms off writing than go through whatever sick punishments Chen has.

The only sounds that can be heard are the scratches of pencils on paper. The crowd of workers stands there, breathless, waiting for us to finish. Their stone eyes bore into my head, reading my thoughts. This is the worst part: humiliation.

"Now, I need you to write confession letters about every single one of your crimes. Afterward, you will read it out loud. You have thirty minutes, starting now. Again, if there is a single wasted space, you know what will happen." Chen's greedy grin reaches across his face as a hungry fire rages in his eyes.

Scrr. Scrr.

The scratches of pencils against paper break the deafening silence.

Tick.

Tock.

Tick.

Tock.

Chen paces, his eyes glued to our papers. Each minute flies by like a falcon diving for its prey.

"Dingdingding. Time's up," Chen sings. "The *clever, disguised* escapee goes first."

And the falcon grips its prey with its knife-like talons.

I stagger forward, my legs feeling like water. My heart pounds as my eyes scan the crowd. The hopeless eyes stare at me as if they are statues.

"I committed my first sin when I was three-"

"Incorrect," Chen cuts in, "You committed your first sin when you were born. Continue."

"The earliest sin I can remember was when I was three years old and stole a slice of apple from my kitchen counter. I ate the whole thing and then stole another piece until I had eaten the whole apple my mother had cut for my father. When I was four, I wet the bed almost daily; when I was five, I was late for school. I lied to my dad when he asked me if I had completed my homework. That was when I was nine," my voice quivers. "I accidentally-"

"There are no accidents," Chen interrupts again.

"I dropped and broke my mother's favorite cup when I was ten and forgot to do my homework a few weeks ago."

Silence.

"That's it?"

"Yes, sir."

"It's a sin to not repent for your previous sins. You haven't written enough. You've been living for over fifteen years. It's impossible that you haven't committed any more crimes. Concealing sins is a sin in itself, especially when you had been ordered to write down *all* of them," Chen explains.

Crack.

A flash of lightning zaps my face. It tingles from where Chen slapped me. I clutch my cheek and a tear streams down my face.

"This is a warning. Next time, write more. You must list *all* of your confessions. A donkey could say more than that when it hasn't even committed as many crimes as you have."

"Yes, sir."

DAY TURNS TO night. It is time for the moon to overpower the sun. But even though it wants to spread justice within its kingdom, darkness comes and unleashes chaos. The moon watches helplessly, shedding tears. The stars burn in fury, far away, as they witness the destruction on Earth. If only they could be set loose to free us from the dark, but they are chained, just like us.

The blanket of sleep hugs me tighter and tighter as my eyes struggle to keep themselves open. Just a little more. Just a little more writing and then I'm done.

Khaaa.

A rock lodges in my throat. Yu is deep in the realm of dreams. If Chen finds out...

"Yu. Yu. Wake up. Yu. Hello? Yu? *Yu?"*

"What?"

"Wake up. You still have two more pages to write."

"Leave me alone. Let me sleep. It's one a.m."

"Yu, I'm serious. Come on. Get up. You can't sleep without permission and you haven't finished Chen's task."

"I want to sleep. Go away."

"Wake up already. Chen will punish us."

"Who gave you two permission to doze off?"

As if this punishment isn't enough.

"Get up. Guards, what do we do with disobedient workers?"

My heart drops into my knotted stomach. We all know the answer.

"Yu, why couldn't you have listened?"

Bruises and fresh cuts are splotched all over our bodies like paint. Our bodies feel skeletonless, spread all over the place. Our bones are cracked and crushed and we feel like jellyfish struggling outside the water.

"I didn't know they would do that. Besides, I was so sleepy that I couldn't understand what was going on. It happens to everyone, even *Chen."*

"Of course, they were going to beat us. That's why we're in here. But we wouldn't be in this state *if you had only listened."*

"This isn't my fault."

"It is. Who else is to blame? *Me?"*

"It's Chen's fault. All of this is his fault," Yu snaps.

"But who provoked him? Oh yeah, *you* did."

"Stop it. It isn't my fault we were beaten. It isn't my fault we're in this place. It isn't my fault for any of this."

"You could have prevented this beating *if you had only listened.* We wouldn't be bruised and bleeding if you had *only listened."*

"It's not like you've never made *any* mistakes in your life."

"This isn't about *me.*"

"Let's stop it, Kai. Enough. Whatever happened, happened. Let bygones be bygones. We can't change the past."

"Really? 'Whatever happened, happened?' What about my parents? What about Hala? All that happened to them is your fault because guess who told the Chinese where we were? If they're dead, their blood is on *your* hands. You're a traitor to everyone."

"Again," Yu mumbles.

My heart thumps with glee upon seeing his face. I can see he's broken. I can see the effect my words had. He sprints away, his sobs carried by the wind.

"He didn't deserve it," The Voice remarks.

He did. After all, he betrayed my family.

"He was forced to. Otherwise, he would be dead. You know it's not his fault. You told him that it was alright a day ago."

It is his fault. You wouldn't understand.

"Apologize. You hurt him for the second time after taking it all back. This time, the damage has been done. At least you don't know whether your family is dead. He saw his parents' corpses."

What about me? Am I not hurt?

"Not everything is about you. Learn to be selfless."

I lay down, stifling my yelps. My whole body feels like it's on fire and throbbing aches course through my veins. Within a minute, my eyes are shut and my mind wanders to another world, one where there is happiness and compassion.

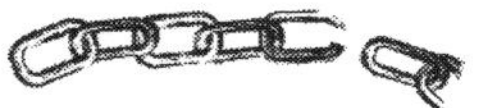

CLANK. CRASH. THUD.

I jump out of my sleep to find orangish-red patches everywhere. Fire? What's going on? I reach around to find something to cover my nose with when my hand grips something wet. I tug at it until the light illuminates the object.

Panic flies right through my heart as I drop the hand. I wipe my hand on the dirt one hundred times but the horror still remains.

My eyes dart from side to side until a realization dawns on me.

Uyghurs fighting the Han.

Chen's men massacring the Uyghurs.

It's a battle.

A dark, familiar flash zooms by. "Yu. *Yu.*"

He looks back for a split second, gazing into my eyes, but he turns and continues running.

"Fight back. Don't let some *Yě shòu* beat you. *We* are their masters," Chen commands. A wave of soldiers surges in and swallows all in their path.

I dive behind a barrel, barely missed by the bombardment of bullets. Seconds pass by like days. All movement slows down to the point that I can see every muscle twitching.

Bullets shower down like rain.
Children scream like thunder.
Bodies collapse like an earthquake.
Blood splatters like a tsunami.
Then silence.
Ghostly, piercing silence.
Fate hovers, laughing.
And then darkness.

Thud. Thud.

The storm unleashed by the guard's footsteps ring in our ears like earthquakes.

Clank. Clank.

The chains rattle in a rhythm, oblivious of the prisoner in its grip.

"You were a part of this revolt, correct?" Chen interrogates.

The light shines on Yu's face, revealing the distorted, swollen flesh. Blood runs down his cheek like rivers and brutal, colorful splotches mask his skin. One of his legs is bent and he leans forward, grasping his ribs. I flinch, the scene engraved in my mind.

"Answer."

"It's not what you think, sir. I was swept into it. I would never-"

"Answer the question, boy."

"No, sir."

"You dirty liar. It doesn't matter. I saw you. You were their leader, correct?"

"No, sir."

"Don't lie to me."

"It's the truth, sir."

"I'm warning you. *Don't lie to me."*

"I'm not lying. I would never revolt, let alone lead a rebellion. Please."

"Hmh, what do you have to say to these prisoners, oh mighty leader?"

"I'm not their leader. I didn't do anything wrong," Yu pleads, the desperation in his voice squeezing my heart.

"Guards," Chen nods. The soldiers line up, their rifles revealed. One throws a dark bag over Yu's face.

"I didn't do anything. I'm innocent. I wasn't the leader. I didn't know what was going on. I was swept into it. I didn't touch a single hair on a soldier. Please, let me go. Please."

Ke. Ke. Ke.

"No, please. Please. *I didn't do anything. Please. Please."*

Clink. Clink.

"Stop. Stop. StopStopStopStop. Please. PleasePleasePlease."

The terror in Yu's voice shakes my heart. My stomach twists and turns and vomit climbs my throat.

THUMPTHUMP.

THUMPTHUMP.

Chen nods and each soldier aims with the monstrous gun in their hands. A disturbing smirk spreads on his face.

Tetetetetetete.

The bullets rip Yu apart. Bone, blood and flesh shoot right out of him. The bag flies off his face and his eyes meet mine, locking for what feels like hours. His eyes beg but I can't move. I am glued to the ground. The fear and agony dance in his eyes right before the life is sucked out of him, his face frozen in a painful trance.

14

ON TÖT

THE EXECUTION KEEPS on playing every time I close my eyes. Yu's hollow eyes float everywhere and the echo of gunshots rings in my ears. It's like a boulder is dragging my heart down to my feet. Sleep has abandoned me like migrating birds flying away. Tears flow out every few minutes like a flashing storm until there is no more water to shed.

Yu's body has been hung in the center of the camp. Chen has put it there intentionally. There isn't a way around it and every time we walk by, Yu's screams can be heard. Even though it's only been a day, Yu's body is bloated and flies buzz around him. A strong, foul smell travels around the camp and vomit hangs in my throat, ready to spill out anytime.

"Time to eat," a monotone, heavy voice calls out through the loudspeaker, interrupting my thoughts.

Regret surges in like a flash flood.

I wish I had been thankful and selfless.

I wish I had been the child Mama and Papa always dreamed of.

I wish I had been a proper older brother to Hala.

I wish I had been nicer to Yu and never yelled at him.

I wish I didn't say what I said.

I wish I had hugged him.

I wish.

I wish.

I wish.

And now, he's

G

O

N

E

It's too late.

It's too late.

The tears pour out again as I drag my feet to the "cafeteria." The other workers buzz around like bees, rushing right past me.

Clank.

Cracked, sticking plates are shoved into everyone's hands, the mud-like mush inside wobbling around. I zone out, swimming in my own head as the line inches forward.

Clank.

A plate is thrown into my hands. I break out of my trance and peer down. My eyes bulge out of my head and my blood goes cold.

Clink. Clink.

The dish vibrates and the liquid swishes as my hands start an earthquake.

"Sit down and eat it," a voice commands from behind me.

"Y...Y...Yes sir."

I robot-walk to the "dining" room, a barren room where every prisoner chews, cramped on the dirt floor. Chen follows me, his eyes drilling through my head. I fall to the ground and glare at the pork and wine. My heart climbs to my throat and threatens to come out.

"This is your punishment. *Eat it."*

None of my muscles obey. I continue gawking at the food.

"Eat it!"

All eyes turn towards me, the same expression glued on each one. My hand grips the meat and slams it into my mouth. Tears drip down my cheeks as I chew. I grab another piece and another and force them down. Bile claws its way up my throat.

"Good boy. Don't forget to drink," Chen smirks.

I gulp the bitter, spicy liquid and my tongue catches on fire. I spit it all out of my mouth without giving it a second thought.

Crack.

Chen's hand strikes like a bolt of lightning and ignites my face.

"Now, make sure not to spit anything out or you won't get any food for a month."

I nod, the tears gushing out now. My head is about to fly away and fog clouds my mind. A giggle slips through my mouth and then, I'm laughing.

Hard.

I laugh like I'm in a palace.

I laugh like Chen never existed.

I laugh like I'm in Heaven.

Chen's smirk grows wider and the fire in his eyes roars.

"Look at this crazy, drunk boy. He's underage and drunk. That is a federal offense. He should be punished for breaking the law on top of his other many crimes."

"If anyone should be punished, it's you. You're a monster. A complete monster who thinks he's better than everyone." I laugh.

I vomit all over the floor, bile coating my clothes and dripping from my mouth and Chen's face explodes.

My eyes flutter open as if waking up from a peaceful nap. I sit up, half expecting an ax to come out of nowhere and chop my head off. But there's only silence and darkness.

No bullet rips through my heart.

No sword explodes from my stomach.

No saw severs my neck.

To make everything stranger, I'm sitting in a chair. Since when has Chen let us sit in chairs? Especially proper chairs?

"Ah, you're awake. How are you feeling? Do you feel nauseous?" Chen appears from the shadows and asks politely.

"I.."

"You can be honest with me, son."

Son? Since when am I his son?

"My stomach is a bit upset, sir," I croak.

"Here," he hands me a harmless-looking, white pill, "Swallow this and you will feel better."

"Thank you, sir."

I shove the pill down with a sip of water. Chen is...being kind. A gentle tingling climbs up my arms. "Am I supposed to be feeling numb, sir?"

"Yes, yes. It's a side effect."

I wait for a few moments, anticipating the bubbling in my stomach to cease. Instead, it just intensifies. My body feels like it's ripping apart from my soul. My brain pounds against my skull and my lungs burn like they're on fire. My stomach climbs into my throat and remains there. The world spins in a spiral and my eyes beg to close. I feel like I'm floating out of my body.

I can't fall asleep. I can't...fall...asle...ep.

I WAKE UP in the same position I blacked out in. All signs of life are gone. The only objects left in the empty room are the chair, the ropes and me. I claw and scratch at the ropes, but they don't budge.

You can't tear snakes apart, can you? The snakes that wait for you to feel helpless and then strike. The ones that squeeze the life out of you and drool at the sight of you go limp. The snakes dig deeper into my wrists, biting at the flesh.

"Are you awake?"

I nod, my head feeling heavy.

"Feeling better?"

"Yes, sir. Thank you, sir."

"It's time to get out now. It's the middle of the night and you've been asleep for a few days. You've made me miss my bedtime."

A few days? What was in that pill?

"I'm sorry, sir."

"Get out."

Chen shakes his head and sighs like he's trying to calm a toddler.

I rush to the building next door.

Today marks the "one-month" anniversary. It's been a month since I've been here. It's been a month since I've seen my family.

And I don't think I'll ever see them again.

"Don't say that," The Voice scolds.

It's a fact. I'll never see them again.

"If you think like that, you'll *actually* never see them."

And then, The Voice disappears.

I make my way through the hallway of cells, cramped with Uyghurs, all sleeping on top of each other. I scan all twenty cells until I find one with room for just one more person.

"Hey, what are you doing?" A deep voice bellows.

"Chen sent me here to go to sleep, sir."

"Well, you can't sleep until your wrists and ankles are tied. Come here."

My eyes didn't even close for a minute. I can feel the shadows around my eyes. My limbs ache with a dull, burning pain, like a lion slowly eating its prey, watching it suffer. The chains tying my wrists to my ankles are finally broken as I make my way to the field. I rub the angry, puffy skin but it only cries thick, red tears. Time to collect a million bags of cotton.

A dark figure shifts and I peer at it from the corner of my eye.

Chen? Why is he staring at me?

My heart begins to *thump* faster as Chen's gaze grows more intense.

Am I doing something wrong? Am I not picking cotton fast enough?

My hands tremble as I stuff cotton into my bag. I try not to look at him but I can feel his eyes drilling into the back of my head.

After what feels like an hour, Chen enters a building. A hushed sigh escapes my mouth.

"Never will we be struck except by what Allah has decreed for us; He is our protector," a voice behind me murmurs.

I turn to find an old man reciting the Quran. His face looks like cloth that was left crumpled and unironed. The white of his beard makes him look like a ghost and his voice trembles. He wheezes heavily with each step, the Earth sucking him in slowly.

"I don't fear anyone but Allah, not even the Chinese government. I've been in this camp for decades and I've survived. I don't have much time left. Besides, I'm going to die sooner or later, so why not die doing good?" the man announces as if he read my mind. "I've lived long enough to know what you people are thinking," he smiles at me, the corners of his mouth rising to the clouds. He huffs and puffs towards me.

"I'm really sorry. I didn't mean to be rude. I...I was just-"

"Curious. That's what people are these days. Curious."

I cast my eyes towards the dirt and start poking it with my toe.

"Don't be shy."

My eyes meet his. A spark of courage shines in his eyes but is quickly covered as if it's a secret.

"I'm Taio, by the way. What's your name?"

"Kai...Kai, uncle."

Taio leans in close. "Now, listen to me carefully. You seem like a nice boy but you must keep this a secret..."

15

ON BESH

THE FADING GLOW of fireflies forms a path into the gloomy forest. The cushiony grass crunches under soft steps and the *crik* of grasshoppers are carried by the whistling breeze. A heavy, wet blanket of air floats down to the dirt, painting it white, while the trees climb higher and higher.

A muddish, woven cloth appears out of nowhere.

Whoosh.

I throw the door aside and step into the cramped shelter. All mouths freeze and all eyes dart towards me, fearful expressions plastered on each face. A little girl playing with a homemade doll drops it and jumps into a woman's lap. The men surround the others, like the walls of a fort closing in, their fists clenched like iron balls.

"He is to be trusted."

Taio hobbles to the front. He clasps my hand. "This is Kai. He will be joining our meetings, if he chooses to do so. He has promised not to mention a word about this to anyone.

Everyone sits back down but they continue scanning me.

"Let's continue. Allah says in the Quran, 'and We made those who had been oppressed succeed to both the east and the west of the land that We had blessed. Your Lord's good promise to the Children of Israel was fulfilled, because of their patience, and We destroyed what Pharaoh and his people were making and what they were building.'

"The Children of Israel were given ease after years of oppression. The boys were slaughtered, the adults were enslaved and every single one of them had to endure Pharaoh's torture. Allah promises us all, the oppressed, that we will be saved soon, whether that be in life or death, as long as we are patient. Trials and hardships are a part of life and it is a test to prove our faith. O Allah, we are waiting eagerly for your salvation and your help. Grant us the patience and strength to survive this oppression. O Allah, You always fulfill Your promises and no matter when Your help arrives, we are grateful for everything You have given us. Please, please, save our people. Don't let all of these innocent children starve, don't let our women get forced into marriage and don't let our men suffer the intense labor. O Allah, protect us from all the harm they inflict on us and grant us Your pleasure."

"Amen," hopeful voices murmur. Even the toddler raises her hands. The floor is soaked with tears as each person lowers their head in humility. A bright energy shines from each person, illuminating the cramped hut until it shines brighter than the moon.

DIM STREAKS OF yellow and orange illuminate the sky, preparing the Earth for the arrival of its new king, the sun. The leaves and grass bow and the wind runs to greet the new ruler. The world erupts with color as the sun embraces everything it can grab.

Crash.

My back slams into the stone wall. The guard yanks me away and slams me again, face first. A *crunch* resonates from my chest.

"What were you doing in the fields?"

"I was working, sir."

"Why did I catch you sleeping then?"

"I...I don't know."

"You. Don't. Know? *Well, this will make you remember."*

He pounds me against the wall, again and again, until my brain wobbles inside my head. Something wet flows down my face until *drip*, it falls to the ground, painting the floor crimson.

"Tell me, why were you sleeping?"

"I don't know. I really don't. I was exhausted. I must have accidentally fallen asleep. Please, forgive me, sir. It won't happen again. I promise."

"Accidentally? There are *no* accidents."

My eyes flutter open with the Earth balanced on my head. My muscles are limp and it feels like I'm floating in the clouds, the sun's warmth soaking into my bones.

...

Floating in the clouds? I jolt awake and a flash of white pain shoots up my ribcage. I collapse back down into the bed, my fists clenched due to the pain. I examine my surroundings, only to grow more confused.

This...this isn't a cell or heaven?

A bent shadow stumbles towards me, a bowl in its hand. The air smells like meat and vegetables.

Like stew warming my insides.

Like fluffy, airy bread.

All the things I can only dream about.

"Eat, little one."

I gulp down the contents of the bowl, taking in every flavor and smell I can.

"You're eating as if you haven't eaten in centuries," the figure chuckles.

"Taio, what am I doing here?"

"You broke your ribs and fainted. I managed to convince Chen to give you a two-day break. After all, an injured worker is no use."

"Thank you."

"Now, rest, my child."

He squeezes my hand gently and begins humming a familiar tune. My mind begins to go numb as my eyelids droop down as the tune takes me to the sky, where only happiness exists.

"Taio, why do you live *here*? Shouldn't you be in the camp?" I ask, gazing at the shadowy, straw ceiling.

"Chen has *some* mercy in him, even if it is a little. Besides, he said I was a danger to the rest of the workers due to my words. But it's not like I live here peacefully. There are security cameras everywhere, inside and out. My every move is monitored and if I do anything wrong, I will be punished."

My eyes dart to the ceiling, catching a glint of light reflecting off a black box.

"I'm aware of all activities in this camp so no matter what you do, I will always know." Chen's ghostly voice echoes in my ear.

"Now, sleep and let me sleep, child," Taio mutters.

"I...can't sleep. Everything hurts."

Umh.

A muffled grunt escapes Taio's mouth as he staggers upward. He makes his way to a wooden chest and pulls out a small jar. "Here," he shoves a cup into my hand, "Drink it and you'll fall asleep."

The second the sweet, warm liquid drains my throat, my head grows heavy and the pain melts away. My eyes droop closed and I collapse in bed.

"WAKE UP. Wake up, child. Time to get back to work."

"I don't want to. Let me sleep."

"No one wants to work but you have to. You have to wake up if you want to live. Now, get up before Chen comes here and makes you."

I roll out of bed the second Chen's name is mentioned. I sprint towards the field and begin tearing the cotton.

I tear.

And tear.

And tear.

Letting the lava inside flow out.

Letting the tears inside pour out.

Letting the grief inside stream out.

As the last cotton ball goes into the bag, Taio hobbles beside me.

"Listen, Kai. I want to ask you something."

"Yes, Taio?"

"I know I only have a few more days left until I...leave but I want to live those days knowing that I am free. I want to leave but I can't escape alone..."

"When do you plan to go?"

"Tonight."

"I..I don't know."

I touch my neck, feeling Chen's talons wrap around it.

Taio's disappointment burns a hole through my heart.

"Where should we meet?"

THUMP. THUMP.

My heart pounds against my ribs as the shadow creeps closer and closer.

If he looks through the hole, he will find us. If he touches the plank, he will catch us. What did I sign myself up for? Why am I trying to escape after what happened last time? If he finds me, I'm dead.

Doubt inches towards my heart as Taio's muffled snores resonate like bellows from a bull.

Khhhha. Khhha.

A bush of black hair spikes out of a merciless face. His eyebrows furrow until they're a shadowy line and his mouth zips into a tight line.

He's found me. He's found me. I can never escape this place. I will never find Hala again. I will never ever experience life outside of here.

Creak.

A plank of wood screams open as the figure peers in. My breath lodges inside the closing dungeon of my throat.

"Hello? Is anyone in he-"

Crack.

My hands tremble.

Clank.

The metal bar drops, deep, chilling vibrations roaring from it. Horror squeezes my heart and my blood freezes.

Chen.

I just hit *Chen* with a *metal rod.*

"Taio, wake up. Wake up. *Wake up.*"

"What? What's going on? Is everything alri-He's not dead, is he?"

"I...I don't know. I don't think so. I couldn't have hit him that hard."

"Check his pulse," Taio commands with such calmness, it almost makes me forget that Chen is here.

The faint *thump* allows the air in my lungs to exhale in peace. The brick in my throat shrinks. Chen isn't dead but we will be if we don't run, *right now.*

THE GRASS CRIES and the twigs scream as the *snaps* echo throughout the still air. The sun peeks out, curious but horrified.

"Come back here. Right now. Before we have to make you. You all are *dead prey.*"

The guards become specks of sand on the horizon as the Earth between us grows. The clank of leashes pierces the air as the hounds bark like sirens.

Whhhe.

Taio grips his knees and wheezes as the barking gets louder and louder.

"Come on, we have to hurry."

"Run without me, son. I'm old now. I'm going to die anyway. You have your entire life ahead of you. Run. I'll only slow you down. My body has failed me now but yours hasn't. Go. Run. Run before you lose the chance. You've made it this far."

"No, I'm not going anywhere without you. I'm not going to leave you. I can't leave you."

A pained smile spreads on Taio's face. He takes a deep breath and his legs chug forward as the trees become dark blurs around us.

Grrrrr.

Grrrr.

GRRRR.

Knives sink into my leg and I tumble onto the ground. The knives sink deeper and deeper until *hiss*, blood pours out of the wound like a waterfall.

Taio stands dazed a few steps ahead of me.

"Go. Go. Taio, go. Go. Go. *GoGoGo."*

He still stands there, shocked.

"Go. Hurry."

He turns and disappears in a flash. A shower of peace rains down on me.

Taio will make it. He will. He has to.

"This stupidity of yours is going to cost you your life. Do you realize that? Just wait until we get back to camp and you will find out what real pain is," a guard threatens.

"It doesn't matter. I'm going to die sometime, whether it be now or later. But remember, you will be judged on the Day of Judgment. On that day, no one can save you. Not Chen, not Xi Jinping, no one."

Smack.

My face snaps backward. A quiet groan escapes as a throbbing ache grows on my face.

"Look at this. A weak, little boy is threatening me with a 'Day of Judgment.' We'll see you on your 'Day of Judgment,' which will begin the instant you get back to where you belong."

16

ON ALTE

KHA. KHA.

I slowly leave the land of nightmares as someone snores beside me.

...

Snoring? I'm supposed to be alone here.

My eyes blink open to find a crinkled face next to mine.

"Taio," I elongate, emphasizing each letter.

"Mmmm."

"Taio?"

"Yes?"

"What are you doing here?"

"What do you think?"

"Were you caught?"

"If I wasn't, why would I be here?"

"But you're not supposed to be here! You had to escape. I'm the only one who should have been caught, not you."

Crash.

The door slams open.

"Whose idea was it?" Chen barks.

Silence.

"Whoever confesses will go free and can leave the country."

"Chen, both of us know you're a liar. Don't expect us to believe that," I blurt out.

"And *you*. What a waste. You wasted your life on this pathetic man. You could have saved yourself if you hadn't run away with *him*."

Chen playfully pokes me with his pistol. The *click* coming from it snaps my mind in two and my blood boils, echoing in my ears.

"If anyone's life is a waste, it's *yours*."

"Only *Gŏu* talk back to their masters. That's what you are. *A dog*. Humans are civilized people who don't believe in a religion that promotes *violence*."

"Don't talk about our faith like that. You don't know anything about it. Islam does not promote violence. It promotes the opposite: peace, justice and respect. Have you seen *any* of us hurt *anyone?* We are people who value law and order. Keep your lies to yourself and *stop this*," Taio bursts.

"We don't need to hear what you have to say, *pathetic, old man.* You have no idea what you're saying. Keep your imagination to yourself."

Chen hungrily glares at Taio.

"Old men are not useful to me. However, *you* are more valuable to me alive."

Alive.

Alive.

Alive.

The words echo in my head. I try to grab onto them, but they continue fluttering around.

Chen nods.

The soldiers ready their rifles.

Aim.

Fire.

And fire.

And fire.

Tetetetetetete.

The helpless man's body crumples to the ground and his limbs twitch as the bullets rip right through him. A sea of blood pours out and by the time the bullets stop, all that's left of him are his empty, glassy eyes.

"YOU HAVEN'T EATEN the food I sent you, hmm?"

I continue staring at the bullet holes in the wall, trying to calm the fire inside me. Dried, crusty blood paints the rooms.

"Answer me."

I shake my head. Words can't form in my mouth without a tear streaming down my cheek.

"You won't get any other food until this plate is wiped clean, even if that means starving to death. Understand?"

I nod, the vein in my neck throbbing.

I will never eat this again. Last time, the food made me feel funny and Chen took advantage of the situation. I will not eat or drink something my religion tells me not to even if I die.

"HELLO?"

A sharp, hushed voice lures me out of my sleep. A tall figure looms in front of the door but all I can see is a blurry blob. I wipe my eyes and let them adjust to the dim light as I sluggishly make my way to the cell door.

"Are you the kid who tried escaping with the old man?"

"Who are you?"

"My name is Liang. I'm Chen's son."

"You're Chen's son?"

I jerk away from the door. "Yeah...He might not be the best person you've ever met."

"Might? He is the absolute *worst* person I've met. Why are you here? Did your father send you? Are you here to kill me?"

"No, no, no. Father was talking about you at dinner and my curiosity got the better of me. That's something I've got to fix before it kills me. Here," Liang hands me something crumbly as he nervously draws with his foot, "It's bread. It's not much but I think it's better than eating something you're not supposed to."

"Why would you care about what I can and cannot eat?"

"I love learning about different religions because I believe it promotes peace," Liang beams.

Huh, there always is the diamond in the coal.

Creeeeak.

"I should be going now. I don't want Father to find out about this. He has anger issues," he begins to make his way towards the door.

"Liang?"

"Yeah?"

"Thanks."

He smiles and nods before the darkness outside swallows him. I gobble the bread down in one bite and the monster inside growls in satisfaction.

Creeeak.

"Who's there?"

17

ON YETTE

"WHO'S THERE? HELLO?"

A tiny head pops out from the wall.

"Who are you? Why are you here?"

"It's best you don't know my real name. It's dangerous in case Chen finds out about what I'm going to say but you can call me Mei."

"You shouldn't be here. It's too dangerous. A soldier can come any second. Leave before it's too late."

"No, the next guard comes in about eight minutes. I have that much time."

"Fine. What are you warning me about?"

"I heard Chen talk about you today. He said, 'I have to get rid of that boy the instant I humiliate him in public. I've been looking for him for *years* and now, he's finally in my grasp. I won't let him get away this time.'"

"What does he mean?"

"I don't know but that's not why I came here. I came here to warn you about the humiliation he was talking about. Four years ago, there was a girl who tried escaping four times but was caught each time. When she was caught the fourth time, Chen was furious. He made her stand in front of everyone and give a speech about the superiority of the Han, abandoning Islam and surrendering ourselves to the government. After that, he...he hung her in front of everyone. Her body hung in the assembly area for weeks until it had completely deteriorated. Chen punished everyone for what she did, claiming that we were all in it. He's going to do the same to you."

A stone lodges in my throat. Her face hardens and she clenches her fists.

"No matter how scary it seems, please, *please,* don't give that speech. Motivate us all. We just need motivation."

"But...but...bu-"

"You haven't been in here long enough. You don't know real pain. Whether you give that speech or not, Chen will make you suffer." She rolls up her sleeve to show a patch of angry, black skin with the word '*Gǒu.*'

My eyes widen in horror.

"I realized after that day that no matter what I did, Chen would hate me. So please, don't think about the pain. Think about the greater good. *Please."*

"But what about my family? What about my sister? I have to find them but I won't be able to if Chen kills m-"

Thud. Thud.

"Mei, get out of here *now.* The guards are coming."

"I can't. There's only one way out."

"Hide. *Hide."*

"I see you haven't eaten the food I gave you," Chen exclaims, a few seconds after Mei is swallowed into a closet flooding with torture weapons.

I force my mouth closed, keeping the response in my head. *I must remain silent. I must remain silent.*

"Don't worry. You won't be my problem after tomorrow."

As Chen's footsteps become nothing but hushed whistles, I glance at the closet. A hushed rustle comes from Mei.

"Excuse me, sir. May I go outside to use the bathroom?" I ask the guard stationed next to the cell door.

"You have a bucket. Use it," the soldier growls.

"It's full. I have to go really badly."

"Fine. I'm only letting you go because Chen wants you alive. Otherwise, I would have my way with you."

The door swings open and I follow the stick-like man outside. I hide behind a few bushes and wait.

This better be enough time for Mei to escape.

"How long does it take to go to the bathroom? Hurry up," the guard booms.

"Coming."

Click.

As the man locks the cell door, I glance at the closet to find emptiness staring back at me. A sigh of relief escapes my lips.

Mei's out.

"ARE YOU WILLING to obey your superiors now?" Chen barks as the first rays of light touch the Earth.

"We're all equal. No one is superior to the other," I mutter.

Chen's eyebrows sink, forming shadows on his eyes. Steam rises from his ears and a bright shade of red colors his face.

"Take him to the assembly," he commands the guards. "Boy, you will regret everything when I get my hands on you. Oh, will I have fun with you," a sick smirk spreads on his face.

The soldiers wrap chains all around me until I look like a metal mummy. I hop to the gathering, each prisoner's empty, hopeless eyes grabbing, clawing for mine. They look like the glass eyes of a doll. A tiny figure nods, her eyes the only ones looking at Chen.

"*Núlì*, this is a *Pàntú* and *Xíngshì*. This animal here deserves to be slaughtered mercilessly. He tried escaping twice and has committed multiple crimes. My sources tell me that he helped that traitor lead the revolt. These crimes will not go unpunished."

"I didn't."

"Shut up. But before death comes what?"

Silence.

"Humiliation. Tell us, *Kai*, how do you feel about your actions?"

I gather all my courage and force it into my heart.

"O people. O fellow prisoners. Who is this man? Who is this man who orders you around? He's our killer. He's out for our souls. He treats us worse than animals. Our suffering is amusing to him. How many fathers, mothers, brothers, sisters and friends have we lost because of those like him? When are we going to stand up?"

"Guards!"

"When are we going to fight for ourselves? Why have we allowed this to happen to us? Why have we allowed them to rip our families away from us? Why have we allowed them to tear our identities away from us?

A sea of arms blocks the sunlight above me.

"O Allah, You are the Most Merciful, the Most Loving. O Allah, save us from the oppressive people like-"

Thwack.

"-You saved Your Prophet. O Allah, compensate us with your reward...for every single person we have lost...O Allah-"

Thwack.

The world melts before my eyes.

"-free us from...the shackles...of humiliation and torture...O Allah, give us back everything we have lost...in the Hereafter...and..."

Thwack.

"Reward."

Thwack.

"Us."

Thwack.

"For."

Thwack.

"Every."

Thwack.

"Suffering."

Thwack.

"We."

Thwack.

"had."

Thwack.

"To..."

Thwack.

"Endure."

The tears race out of my eyes. Hala's last words echo throughout the land.

"Ürkesh. Ürkesh. *Ürkesh."*

Crack.

"You insolent dog. You snake. How dare you? *How dare you?* I *will* make you bow down to me, even if I have to *cut your head off* to do it. *Do you hear me?"*

An iron hand finds its way to my face, lighting it on fire. The pain sears through my skin and bone. Chen grabs my hair and rips it out, fistfuls of dark, clumpy strands gliding to the floor. A wet streak flows down my face, dripping on my clothes, painting them red. My eyes freeze, glued to Chen's. My mouth hangs loose and white-hot pain ripples through my bones.

"This is just a little of what you will experience. I've been nice to you so far, *boy,* but take my word, you will wish you were never born. You will be beaten, starved and tortured until my heart is content. Then I will kill you."

My stomach twists into a million knots. The fire on my face roars all over my body and a puddle of crimson stains my clothes and the stone floor. Chen storms out of the building, each *thud* from his footsteps rattling the earth like an earthquake.

"HEY LIANG, I want to tell you something," I mutter a few hours later as he wipes the blood away and tries to extinguish the fire burning through my skull. A cool liquid is squirted onto my wounds.

"You can tell me anything."

"After...Y...Yu died, it was hard for me to trust anyone but after meeting you, I realized that not all people are cruel. I realized that, despite your father being Chen, you are his complete opposite. I thought all Han citizens were against us. But...I was wrong. I should never have assumed that."

He smiles so wide, it could stretch across the horizon.

"You know, you're my only friend. School's been tough and my father is not the best person to be around. I've always felt lonely until I met you. I realized that you all aren't like my father describes you."

Liang springs from his position and pulls me tight in an embrace. My back automatically jerks and my heart races but after, I wrap my arms around his scrawny body. It's hard to believe he's Chen's son with him being a few inches shorter than me. Liang stays in that position for what feels like hours as my heart beats,

I.

Wish.

This.

Could.

Last.

F o r e v e r.

"What is going on here?"

18

ON SEKKIZ

BOTH OF US flinch when we hear that deep, booming voice.

Chen.

Chen is here.

I turn, finding the snarling beast. Its eyes glow red and its fangs glint in the faint light. Its claws grow sharper and longer each second while drool drips down the side of its mouth.

"Dad-"

"Don't you *dare* 'dad' me. I don't need to hear your silly excuses. My own *son* befriends a Uyghur, a *Bèndàn*. What am I going to tell the government when they find out?"

"Ple-"

"*What did I just say? Don't give me any excuses.* You had *one* job. *One* and you failed. You *failed* as a son."

Chen snatches Liang's wrist and swipes him off his feet, sending the boy flying towards him. I lunge at his other arm and pull him in the other direction, his hand slipping off Liang.

"Wha-"

"Back off."

"What did you say?"

"I said back off. Get your hands off him."

"He's *my* son, *Móguǐ*. I can do whatever I want with him."

"Kai, please don't," Liang pleads under his breath, his eyes brimming with tears.

Chen reaches out and smashes Liang into the wall, a river of blood trickling down his face. Chen pants like a starved, bloodthirsty lion.

"You are no better than them. How dare you go directly against the orders of your own father? How dare you?"

I pounce on Chen from behind. He flinches and the fire in his eyes turns into surprise, only to ignite again. He snarls and bites like a rabid animal.

"Stop it. Leave your poor son *alone*. He doesn't need to deal with the devil."

Chen throws me off, scrambling to Liang. He lifts the boy by his neck, his iron hands squeezing. Liang twitches and claws at his father's hands and his eyes bulge out before he goes limp. Chen jerks him and slams him into a chair, splintering it into a million pieces.

As Chen's feet come to life, I pounce on him again.

"Do you realize what kind of a father you are? Do you? *You're a despicable, corrupt father to a kind-hearted son. Your son didn't fail, you did."*

Chen freezes into an ice statue as the poison spraying from my mouth empties. I let go of his crumpled shirt as he melts onto the floor. I watch as his tongue twists and turns, only slurred sounds coming out of them.

A dark figure catches my attention.

Liang.

I rush to him. "Liang. Liang. You're father's okay now. He isn't a monster, at least, not right now. You can wake up. Liang? *Liang? Wake up. Liang."*

I turn him around until I gaze into his hollow, frozen eyes.

"NoNoNoNoNoNo."

I cup my ear over his chest, trying to hear one beat.

Just one.

But all that's left is a

Sad,

Lonely,

Dead heart.

I've lost so much in the past few weeks.

Mama,

Papa,

Hala,

Yu,

Taio,

And now Liang.

RRRRRRRR.

The fire takes over.

I raid the cabinet until I pull out some jars.

"What have you done?"

Smash.

The glass explodes on the ground, scattering like stars in the night sky.

"You killed your own son."

Smash.

"How could you do that?"

Smash.

"How could you kill your child?"

Smash.

"You killed your own blood with your own bare hands. How? How can you do that? Tell me? How?!"

I storm into my cell, slamming the door behind me. Liang's key *clinks* to the stone floor.

A human like Chen doesn't deserve to live.

I look around the cell for something, anything that could hurt Chen.

"I want to kill you like you murdered him, do you hear me?"

"What are you doing? Just because Chen is a devil doesn't mean you should kill him. You'll be just as bad as he is," The Voice warns.

A slow splatter begins in my heart.

"You deserve to do so. I've hurt you so much throughout these months. It's the least I deserve," Chen mutters, his barren eyes fixed on his son.

"What...what do you mean?"

"You haven't been told."

"I haven't been told what?"

"Liang wasn't just your friend. He was your half-brother because I...I am your father."

19

ON TOQQUZ

"YOU'RE A LIAR."

"I mean it from the bottom of my heart."

"Why do you expect me to believe *you?* You're a liar. You've always been one. Not a single word you say is true."

"Kai, I mean it. You *are* my son. I swear by your God."

No.

No.

No.

"Oh yeah? How did my mother marry a *monster* out of all the people in the world? You don't even believe in my God."

"She didn't *want* to marry me. She was forced to."

"I don't believe you. My mother wouldn't let herself be forced into marriage, let alone to you."

"I'm telling the truth," Chen begs.

"Prove it."

Silence.

"Prove it."

He darts out of the building. A few minutes later, he arrives with a paper in his hands. He shoves the document through the cell bars.

Me, Kai, the son of Fu Chen and Chi Lin.

Chi Lin, *my mother.*

Chen *is* my father.

The birth certificate shakes as I hand it back to Chen. The words keep repeating in my head like a gong.

Chen is my father.

Chen is my father.

Chen is my father.

The drizzle turns into fire.

"Tell. Me. Everything. Now."

Chen stares hard at the place Liang was. Now, only a few streaks of red remain.

"Lin and I lived in the same town. We attended the same schools until it was time to go to college. For years, I hadn't seen her until I came back to my hometown to visit my parents. When I was walking to their house, I saw Lin for the first time in years. She had grown into a beautiful, young woman by then. I wanted to marry her, so I confronted her a few days later. I asked if she would marry me, and she bluntly refused. I left her alone from then on. A year later, I came again, this time for business. At the time, all I could think about was our marriage. I asked her again but she refused."

"What did you do afterward?" I ask, breaking the silence.

"I...I threatened to kill her and her family. It was only after the threats that she agreed. Two years later, you were born. The instant I saw you, I hated you. You looked like a Uyghur and I hated that. Your mother sensed that, I suppose, and ran away a week later. I searched for her but couldn't find her anywhere. But as soon as I saw you I knew you were her son."

"If you hated me, you hated her too."

"No, I loved her with my whole heart."

"Did you ever lay a hand on her?"

Silence.

"Did you?"

"I may have hit her a few times but only because she was a stubborn woman. Her rebelliousness needed to be under control."

Red-hot lava seeps into my mind, my eyes only seeing red.

"I guess Liang's not the only one whose father is a devil."

Crash.

I jerk backward to find the beast inside Chen revealing itself. The red, glowing eyes. The blood-soaked fangs. The knife-like claws. His talons wrap around the iron bars separating us.

"You Yě sh..."

Suddenly, the rage drains out of his face.

“I'm sorry, I shouldn't have exploded."

Jing. Jing.

Chen fiddles with the keys and *click*, the door throws itself open to reveal the towering man behind it. He inches close until there is only a foot's gap between us. He raises his arms and I look away, my hands shielding my face from whatever harm he plans on committing. But that blow never comes.

Instead, a pair of warm arms wrap around me, pulling me into a bear hug. My face slams into his stomach, slowly smothering me.

"It's about time to put the past behind us, son," Chen whispers in my ear.

Son.

Son.

Son.

The word rings in my heart and something squirms inside it. A wave of disgust splashes through me and I try to break away from him but Chen’s arms grow tighter and tighter like a vine snaking upwards.

His hand reaches behind his back.

Grabs a dark object.

And before I have any time to react, he cackles.

Bzzzz.

HALA

A FEW WEEKS AGO

20

YIGIRME

"ÜRKESH. ÜRKESH. ÜRKESH."

A wave of arms pulls me deeper and deeper into the sea of people. I claw, bite, scream, twist and turn but it's all useless against the sharks.

Soon, the ground drops and I stand in the air. Blindly, I kick and punch, the desperation inside building until it rips me apart.

"Stop," a slurred voice commands.

My muscles turn into stone and I gulp for air. My arms stop aimlessly reaching and my legs stop thrashing.

Krrrrrr.

My head jerks forward as the guard rips the blue cloth off my head. Torn patches glide down to the ground as a handful of black strands float away, riding on the wind. The rest of my hair unfolds, reaching to my waist as the guards laugh.

I feel so

e x p o s e d.

Everyone's eyes drill into mine.

You're not going to cry. You're not going to cry. Don't let them see you cry.

The tears retreat into the dam.

I dangle in the air.

The guard's face grows crisp.

"Uncle," I mutter, stretching each letter. My mind explodes.

His eyes fall out and an upside-down 'U' stretches on his face. Glum, dark shadows encompass his eyes and bluish-purplish splashes are painted on his face. The once lush bush of hair is now nothing but a few strands and all the muscle and fat have evaporated. He looks like an...alien.

"Uncle. Shan."

"I'll handle her."

The other guards disperse until the silence echoes. "I'm sorry."

"What are you doing? Why are you wearing a soldier's uniform?"

"I was forced to. He made me."

"What are you doing?"

"He made me his assistant under the threat of death."

"But...isn't death better?"

"I'm sorry."

"Isn't death better than doing this to your own people? To your own family?"

"I didn't have a choice. You're too young to understand."

"No, I understand perfectly. My *own uncle* is helping the government against his own people."

"Hala, watch who you're talking to. Respect your elders."

"I'm talking to a concentration camp supervisor."

The color drains out of his face and the upside-down 'U' grows even larger. His bottom lip drops just a little and his eyes look like they will pop out. He releases me and I dive face-first into the dirt.

Diiiiii. Diiiiiii.

Another wave of people floods into an open area. I'm swept without a choice. Uncle steps onto a platform with a shorter man. Black hair is combed neatly on his head and his dark eyes pull everyone into a trance. Light spots dot his face and an almost transparent pair of glasses rest on his nose.

"There are some new 'recruits' to this camp. Let's introduce ourselves to them." A mischievous grin flashes on the man's face. "My name is Bao, and I am your master. This is Shan, my assistant."

Uncle's face twists.

"Now, time for some Q and A. What do we do here?"

"Work," a dull chorus of people responds.

"Good. We have some *young* workers here who need more explanation about their jobs. What kind of work do we do?"

"Any work the glorious Bao gives us," the chorus responds.

"And what happens if someone doesn't work?"

"That person deserves to be punished in any way Bao wishes since he or she disobeyed their master."

"Good. Good. What do young children do in these 'reeducation facilities?'"

"Boys work in the fields. Girls make thread and cloth and they sew."

"Good. What are you all supposed to be doing?"

"Working to help the Chinese become the world superpower."

"Now then, *get to work.* You've already wasted enough time. You may all go into your cells for a *restful* night"

Uncle helps me limp to a dusty cell full of workers. Each one looks like a skeleton, the life slowly fading from them. Some are streaked with red, blue and purple while others' faces are molded into contorted shapes. Whimpers echo in the room and dried blood clumps on the floor.

My heart climbs to my throat as all the eyes turn toward me. Uncle gently nudges me into the cell and locks the door. His eyes fill with water and within a flash, he's gone.

The prisoners cramp into each other, making a few inches of space for me. They look at me with weak, hollow eyes, struggling to keep their smiles from shattering into a million pieces. I smile back.

At least not all the people in this camp are predators.

Within seconds of lying down on the stone floor, everyone circles around me, blocking the prison door from my view, as if protecting me from the horrors that lurk outside.

The stars weakly smile at me as the moon cries, its fiery tears crashing against the Earth. The darkness takes pity and throws a blanket over me. The crickets sing their gloomy songs until the darkness embraces me in its warmth.

21

YIGIRME BIR

CREEEEEEEAK.

"Get up, *Núlì.* Today, we have a special procedure. You all know what to do."

At the sound of Bao's words, everyone jolts out of their sleep and runs out like cheetahs, only to freeze once they're out of the cell. "If anyone moves, they will be sent to the Black Room. Understand?"

"Yes, master," empty voices reply.

Tick.

Tock.

Tick.

Tock.

The watch on Bao's wrist clicks and clicks as he circles around us, his eyes scanning for any movement.

10,070; 10,071; 10,072...10,087-

Ugha. Ugha.

"Well, well. Who do we have here? The rest of you are dismissed."

Thud.

Bao slams the fallen woman into the wall, a snap coming from her back. He coils his arm and strikes like a snake, again and again and again until her eyes are barely open.

"Wait, sir. I...I can deal with her. You are a busy man and this woman is just distracting you from your other duties," I mumble.

Bao smirks like a sly fox and drops the woman. "You have two minutes," he snarls.

I drop to my knees, sitting the skeleton up. The rings under her eyes shadow the rest of her face and her cracked lips drip blood. Her gray skin makes her look like a foreign creature and her shallow breathing making a deep, scratchy noise.

"Please, get up."

"I can't," she croaks.

"If you don't, Bao will kill you."

"I'll either die because of the sickness, Bao or work. It's all the same in the end. Death is going to come to all of us at some point."

"But-"

Thud. Thud.

"It seems like you *failed* the task. It's fine. I expected that from a *new detainee.* Go and start your real work and let me handle this. You don't have the *expertise* to get this pig off the ground."

"Uhh...I was thinking, umm...if you let this woman rest, I...I could do her share of the work."

"Go ahead," he dares.

I stare, wide-eyed, at the skyscraper in front of me. Two hundred pairs of gloves. The pile reaches to the ceiling, blocking the dim light. I snatch the needle and stitch.

And stitch.

And stitch.

Until I can't feel my hands anymore.

But the skyscraper has only shrunk halfway.

Only halfway down and the sun is going to sleep.

"You're still working," a booming voice announces.

I jump in my seat and nod.

"Why did you offer to do that woman's work?" Uncle asks.

"Because it was the right thing to do."

"You still shouldn't have offered. Bao could have killed you. You should be grateful he decided to have mercy on you."

"Sometimes, the right thing to do is the most difficult choice to make."

"I understand that you are upset but you have to listen to me, Hala. I know this place and the condition we're living in *better* than you do. You have to trust me."

"How am I supposed to trust someone who is helping Bao, a camp supervisor?" I snap.

"I was *forced* to. You have to understand. This isn't my fault. At least I'm here so I can help Bao stay away from you. It's the silver lining in this scenario."

"You came all the way here to tell me this?"

He sighs. "You always were the smart one. I came to inform you..."

Silence.

"Came to tell me wha-"

"I killed her," a deep voice interrupts.

"What?" I blurt.

"I killed her," Bao says, slyly.

Bao.

Killed.

Her.

I fight the tears, sucking them back in and begin sewing like a robot. The anger threatens to boil over and my blood starts to bubble.

"Aren't you going to bow, my dear," he coos.

"I'm sorry, master." I bow, my hair covering my humiliated face.

"That's more like it. Keep working on those gloves. You'd better complete them if you want to sleep tonight. Shan, come with me."

Distant murmurs perk my ears.

Don't eavesdrop. Finish your work.

But I have to know what they're talking about. What if it's important?

It can't be that important and definitely not worth your life.

I need to know.

I tiptoe to the door and cup an ear over a crack.

"You still haven't completed what I told you to do. You were supposed to do this *yesterday,"* a stern voice scolds.

"I'm sorry, master. I just-"

"Don't. Make. Excuses. That's all you barbarians do. Now, go and get rid of the prisoners. *Tonight."*

"But-"

"Don't you dare 'but' me. You'd better do the job, Shan, or else I'll *kill* you just like you will kill them."

"Isn't there someone better to do the job," Uncle pleads.

"I've already told you," Bao sighs annoyingly, "I gave *you* this job, no one else. You'd better complete this task. Now, stop arguing."

"Yes, master." Uncle's chin points to the ground and his eyes glue themselves to his feet. He forces his hands behind his back, where they rub against each other. Bao motions towards the door.

I spring back into my spot and grip a needle as two faces appear from the room. The ghostly face remains as the irritated one leaves.

"I'm going to have to monitor you for a while. Bao isn't happy with you...courage," Uncle announces.

Uncle leans down to my ear. "Listen, I need you to warn some people. Bao wants to murder them tomorrow but you can help them escape. Once you're in the cell, ask for prisoners six, nine, thirteen and sixteen. Here's a master key. Tell them to use it but make sure to bring it back, got it?"

"But how-"

"You have to do it, Hala. You can save these people's lives."

I nod, the boulder in my heart sinking.

"WHERE ARE PRISONERS six, nine, thirteen and sixteen?"

Four workers raise their hands, three women and a man.

"Bao wants to kill you all. You must escape *tonight."*

"But how?" the man whispers.

"Here. Use this. But remember, to bring it back. We don't want Bao to find out."

I shove the master key into his scraped hands and watch as they disappear into the dark hallway. A few minutes later, he rushes back and throws the key into the cell.

A deep sigh exits my tight lungs.

"Why would Bao want to kill those four and not all of us?" a prisoner asks.

"I heard they're part of a Uyghur resistance group," a woman responds.

A resistance group? That's what we need here. Soon, we could stop government operations and free everyone.

"How about we make our own in this camp?" I offer.

"Make our *own* resistance group? It's too risky. Besides, Bao has eyes everywhere. If he finds out, he will kill us *all*," the woman remarks.

"The girl's right. We have to fight if we want to live. That's the only way to survive here," a man agrees.

"But all of us have to promise not to tell *anyone* about this, even under threat of death. It doesn't matter if you want to join or not, you must swear not to say a word about this," I announce.

"We promise," everyone replies, their powerful energy glowing during this moonless night.

22

YIGIRME IKKI

"HURRY, WE ONLY have three minutes."

A wheeze comes out of the man. "The prisoners made it to the encampment safely. So far, there aren't any signs of the Chinese. When is the next batch coming?"

"Tomorrow night. Be ready for them."

As soon as the last word rolls off my tongue, the man vanishes, as if the forest has eaten him.

The sky grows murkier as the black streaks begin pouring in. The crisp air tickles my face and the purple and blue splotches on my hands begin to fade into a brownish-yellow shade. The breeze hums a sad tune, lulling me to sleep and the birds chirp their songs.

It's been a week since I've been warning prisoners and constant worry sits in my head.

Bao can find out any minute and then, in a blink of an eye, I will be killed.

I make my way back to the building. The movement of my cellmates creates a hushed *bzzzzz*, blocking all other sounds out as the darkness springs out of nowhere.

CRACK.

Orange and red blurs dance before my eyes as bloodcurdling screams ring throughout the building. Lumps of charred flesh are scattered all over the stone floor. A river of heavy, dark smoke wanders around, blinding me. The heat lashes out and bites at my face, daring me to do something. My head throbs as if a hammer is pounding it mercilessly.

I race to the door, tears stinging my eyes. I grab for the handle but *hissss*, the heat sears my hand.

Crash. Crash.

I slam into the door, again and again.

Please open. Please open.

Slosh.

My foot slips on something thick but liquidy. I bend down, examining the gooey, murky liquid. I sniff it and the realization hits me like an explosion.

Thump.

Thump Thump.

THUMP THUMP.

THUMPTHUMP.

Gasoline.

The liquid is gasoline.

The Han really, really want us dead,

They were the ones who set this fire.

Desperation soars through my heart as my blood freezes.

There must be something, anything that can open the door.

Crrrrrr.

The fire bites at me as my hands search for anything useful.

A scalding object brushes my hand. I claw at the metallic object.

Keys.

I jam one in.

Then the other.

And the other.

And the other.

But nothing happens.

I reach for the last key, only to find the first one again.

The guards took the fifth key.

They trapped us in here.

They set this whole thing up.

The salty water in my eyes finally pours out.

There has to be a way out.

Clank.

My hands dig around until a scratchy, burning block brushes against me. I reach for the long object and smash it into the doorframe.

Creak.

Creeeak.

CREEEEEEEEAK.

The wood splitters into a million pieces and the door screams open.

I run.

And run.

And run.

Until the coolness of the air comforts me. I dash behind a shack and gaze at the crackling flames.

Bao stands near the barbed fence, gazing at the bright, vicious fire, smirking. Hunger runs through his eyes and cruelty shines around him like he himself is on fire. His arms fold across his chest and he spreads his feet far apart, his eyes still glued to the raging orange in front of him.

Crash.

Poof.

The building collapses, put into an eternal sleep but Bao keeps on watching.

And watching.

And watching.

Not caring for those buried in flames. Not caring for those still screaming inside.

23

YIGIRME ÜCH

"NONE OF YOU will get any sleep until you clean this place up. Now, Get. To. Work."

The survivors swarm like bees around the black building, picking up the debris little by little. The mountain slowly grows into a hill as chunks of the roof are passed around until they are dumped into the truck. The smoking pieces of the walls roast our hands, streaks of ashed red brushed onto our skin.

Huuuuuh.

Our heads perk up at the hushed gasp.

"Bodies."

"Bodies."

"Bodies."

The word spreads like a virus.

"It doesn't matter what's under the debris. You have to clear it all up. The longer you take, the longer you're going to have to stay awake," Bao calls out, his arrogant smirk plastered on his face.

Everyone freezes, becoming statues at the sound of his amused voice.

"Hurry up. I don't have the rest of my life to watch you all stand there like chickens."

The statues suddenly jump to life, the *bzzzzzz* echoing through the air once again. The clumps of distorted, scorched flesh tremble in everyone's hands. Torn legs, ripped arms and charred bones surface as the hill turns into a pile. A smokey smell rubs into us while our hands are painted black.

Grrrrrrr.

A deep, threatening growl comes from right behind me.

Rar. Rar.

"What's wrong?" Bao coos, as if expecting the hound to answer.

Grrr.

"Are you hungry?"

Rrr.

"You want that one, hm? No one is stopping you. Go ahead."

Cla. Cla.

Bao claps and everyone turns into stone again.

Smack.

He kicks the dog in the rear.

Grrrrr.

A dark blur races past and tackles the man a few feet ahead of me. It sinks its jaws into his neck and violently shakes his body.

"Aaaah.

"Aaaaah.

"Aaaaaaaaaaaaaaaaaaaah."

Crunch.

The dog bites into his face until deep, red holes are all that are left.

It tears and tears until it's satisfied.

It chews until only thick crimson is layered on the ivory bones.

My eyes remain fixed on the remains as my heart sinks deeper and deeper into my stomach. My guts twist and turn until everything's a jumbled, knotted mess. My joints clatter against each other and my feet glue themselves to the floor.

I finally tear my eyes away and look at the other prisoners. They continue their work as if nothing happened but their hands tremble, earthquakes echoing from them.

BEEEEEP. BEEEEP.

The *bzzzzz* begins anew after the siren goes off and everyone jumps from their light sleep. Stale, moldy bread is tossed into our hands and I glare as everyone devours it.

You don't have a choice. This is all you're going to get all day.

I cautiously nibble the bread, swallowing my disgust. It tastes like socks and dirt.

Don't spit it out. Don't spit it out.

I swallow the last bit, trying to keep the vomit at bay.

"Get to work, *Núlì.* No more food until the building is complete," Bao barks.

Once he's out of earshot, muffled whispers circle around.

"Half of us can build while the other half can bring bricks and cement. Once both groups get tired, we can switch," a prisoner suggests.

Everyone nods and separates into two masses. Without a second to think, the wave of people sweeps me to the supply group. We make a belt, stretching from the bricks to the construction site.

Each brick travels through a sea of arms, finally reaching its destination, after a few minutes. The pile eats and eats until it is a hill after hours of swinging bricks around. My arms feel heavy and swollen as each new brick adds more weight to them.

Meanwhile, the foundation of the new building is barely sprouting from the ground. Bao inspects it, eyeing each stone, a disappointed frown glued to his amused face. The hill of materials becomes a mountain as the last brick travels to its companions.

Both groups then merge into each other, like two waves joining to form a colossal one. We flood the site, throwing cement on the bricks.

"We can leave tonight through the path," some whisper.

Automatically, my eyes search for Bao.

"Hey, I think it would be better to discuss *nature* later. *This*," my eyes point towards Bao, "isn't the right place and time, especially since we are supposed to be working. Talking for fun during a very important job isn't a good idea."

Within a second, everyone's mouths zip up and a deafening silence wraps around the site.

"Hmh."

Bao scoffs and pulls Uncle towards him. As Bao's mouth moves, Uncle's eyes find mine, his face draining of all color.

"WE NEED MORE cement. Does anyone know where to find some?" a woman asks.

"There's a truck full of it. I'm sure Bao... m-master won't mind," another woman responds.

"But who's going to get it? We *all* can't go."

A deadly silence falls between us.

"I'll go," I offer.

"No. You're a child. Let someone older go."

"It doesn't matter. I'm harder to notice."

Everyone's eyes stare at the dirt and they swarm around until they form a wall between me and the guards. I spy Bao talking to a soldier and dart to the truck, repeatedly scanning behind me. Within seconds, a container overflowing with cement is on the ground.

Crash.

I ram right into a rock.

What was that? It wasn't there a few seconds ago.

As my eyes focus, a pompous smirk appears. Bao's smirk.

Thump.

Thump. Thump.

ThumpThump.

THUMP.

THUMPTHUMP.

"What are you doing?"

I bow low. "I was getting more cement."

"I didn't hear you. Say that one more time."

A boulder lodges in my throat. "I was getting more cement, m...ma...master."

"Did you ask me?"

My blood freezes.

"N...no, master."

"Aren't you supposed to?"

"I'm sorry, master."

He roughly grips my shoulder and I freeze as if I have turned to ice, squeezing the container as if my life depends on it.

"Next time, don't do *anything* without my permission. *Understand?"*

"Ye...Yes...Yes, sir."

"Good, now get going."

He shoves me into the container.

Thud.

The metal bucket flies to the ground, its contents spilling out. Bao's smirk flashes into a smile.

"Oh, I'm so sorry. I didn't mean to hurt you."

I tighten my jaw and rub my teeth together, trying to keep the lava from flowing out. I snatch a shovel and throw the dirt-infested cement back into the container.

If it was up to me, I would throw it back into the truck but with Bao, it's better safe than sorry.

After ten minutes, the ground is clean. I drag the cement to the construction site, everyone's eyes drilling into my back.

"How long does it take to build a *prison?* Come on. It's been five days. *Five.* Just make it ugly and weak, no one cares. It's a prison after all. Even dogs can build faster than you all can," Bao whines, walking in circles around us.

As if flipping a switch, everyone goes into turbo mode, throwing bricks on top of each other as their arms move in blurred circles. However, by the time it's a few feet tall, the entire thing collapses, falling like an old man.

"Núlì. You can't even make a building without making it fall? What kind of animals are you?"

Without a single second's hesitation, everyone grabs the fallen bricks and lays them out again, splashing them with cement. This time, the prison cracks like a three-century-old man dying. As we reach out to begin again, the lava inside me explodes, spilling out.

"If we do it slowly and properly, the building won't collapse. That way, we won't have to spend the rest of our lives building."

The workers look at me with their pitiful eyes, begging for a way out of this.

Bao's chuckle turns everyone into ice.

"You're seriously going to listen to a *child?* What kind of dogs are you? Stand back, *girl,* and let the adults do the work *properly*. I have *other* work for you. Shan, you know where to take her."

Uncle's face drains like a bleached cloth. He flinches but suddenly snaps out of his trance, his booming footsteps cracking the ground. He snatches my wrist and leads me away from the site until the workers are specks in the sun.

"Bao's suspicious," Uncle whispers.

“About what?”

“He didn’t tell me but please, please, be very careful.”

I nod and I rewatch as the scene plays in my mind.

"Uncle, why did your expression change when Bao told you to take me somewhere?"

"You noticed that?"

"Yep."

"Wow, I didn't-"

"You didn’t know because you don't know anything about me or my family."

"But your moth-"

"You didn't know *anything* about her. You never cared. You never visited. I can count the times you came over on one hand. Do you know how much she cried, if we even mentioned your name?"

"I didn-"

"You didn't know. You didn't know anything because you never cared about us."

An awkward silence descends.

"You're right. I should have visited more often. I should have tried connecting with my family. I'm so, so sorry," Uncle confesses.

A few beaded tears stream down his face.

"I'm sorry. I shouldn't have gotten mad. You're family after all."

"No, no. You're right. You were right about my current job too. I shouldn't have. But now, I can't quit because I'm afraid for you."

"Thanks for being here, Uncle."

He grins, shining like the sun itself. His face glows, radiating everything around us. But then, a shadow arrives and blocks his emerging light.

"We're here."

24

YIGIRME TÖT

AS MY EYES adjust to the light, tiny, scattered objects appear in the dark.

"What is this place?"

"It's where Bao...does...*certain* things," Uncle sputters.

"What do you mea...Oh."

I can feel my lungs contracting,

My heart racing,

My throat closing,

And the knots in my stomach growing tighter and tighter, squeezing.

And squeezing.

And squeezing.

Cla. Cla.

A bunch of bulky objects are shoved into my arms. The *clank* and *clatter* push me back into reality. I look back towards Uncle, who nods slowly.

The faster you finish, the better.

The white dots of teeth and the beige shine of fingers are spread on the ground like stars. Stars I can pluck out of the sky and put in a bag, where the darkness swallows them.

Those stars belonged to real people. Innocent people killed for no reason.

The bodies come next. Bumps of distorted flesh clumped together to form unrecognizable shapes as if a lion chewed on them.

"What am I supposed to do with...these, Uncle?"

He calmly makes his way towards me and when he lays eyes on the corpses, he stares. He breaks away after a few seconds and disappears into the light.

"Here," he shoves some sacks into my hands, "Put the bodies in these bags."

The boulder in my throat sinks deeper as I throw one body.

And another.

And another.

Into individual bags.

By the time the last body is in a bag, the moon's reign has begun. The darkness sets in, drinking all the color.

Laying on the stone floor amidst hundreds of prisoners, the loneliness eats at me, like a wolf feasting on its prey. The tears constantly break out of their dam, only to be forced back in.

The way the bodies felt is branded on my hands. Their blood can never, ever come off. I wipe my hands on the floor but I can still feel it.

The jingling of keys and the booming, threatening laughter scare the sleep out of me.

Before Bao comes to wake everyone up, I am already awake and leaning against the cell door, trying not to fall asleep. The endless night only gifted me one hour of rest and my limbs are eager to get out of this cramped room.

"I see you've adjusted to the schedule."

"Yes, master."

I look away, trying not to get trapped in his deadly trance. "Look at me."

I force my chin up, locking with his devilish eyes. "You are a strong girl. Why don't you join my troop of *favorable Wéi wú ĕr réng?"*

"No."

Bao turns into a tomato.

"What did you say?"

"I'm sorry...master but I can't join your team. You see, I'm just a *little* girl, a weak one. I'm not strong like you or your assistant. No one would listen to me."

He glares into my eyes as if reading my thoughts. "I would make everyone listen to you."

"It wouldn't help with anything. No one would respect me, even with the authority that comes with such a position. I'd rather use my energy to strengthen China."

"Your choice. If you ever reconsider your decision, please be sure to tell me."

"Yes, sir. Thank you for your *kindness."*

I'd rather burn in a fire or drown than accept his offer. He should understand that.

"YOU ALL HAVE make-up work to complete due to your break," Bao announces.

Each one of us examines the mountain of unstitched gloves.

If the fire was a break, I have no idea what real work is.

My hands hum their usual tune, synchronizing with the other worker's humming. The anger and dread rage on inside, zooming through my veins. My blood boils as the bubbling pot explodes.

A lone tear drips down my face. I can see them in front of me.

Ürkesh reading his textbook, his soul immersed in the sea of words.

Mama placing the bread in the oven, her smile lighting the house.

Papa sipping his tea and glancing over the newspaper, his deep laugh echoing, even in the darkest corners of the house.

A sharp, tingling feeling stabs my finger. I snap out of my trance, watching as the scarlet drops drip onto my shirt and place my finger into my mouth but continue sewing.

And sewing.

And sewing.

Another tear streams down my cheek but I wipe it away before anyone notices.

You can't be weak. That's what they want. Don't give them what they want.

"How's it going?"

Why does Bao have to bother me out of everyone in the entire room?

"Thank you for allowing me to work for the Chinese, master."

"How many pairs have you completed?"

"Three, sir."

"Why so little in so much time?"

"I'm sorry."

"Say that again. I can't hear you."

"I'm sorry, master."

"Hmh, do you need help?" He raises his eyebrows.

No, I don't.

"That would be an honor, master."

"Oh, I just remembered. I have an important meeting in a few minutes. Please, excuse me. I will come back to help as soon as I'm free. Being a supervisor is hard work.." His sly smirk widens as he turns to walk out the door.

I hope he never comes back.

"WAKE UP," a soft voice says. A gentle hand shakes my shoulder, forcing my eyes to open.

"Hurry, get back to work before Bao comes," the woman warns. Her skin shines in the dull light and her deep, dark eyes twinkle. Her long, smooth hair goes down to her waist. Even with the purple streaks and red gashes, she is beautiful.

A muffled groan slips as my eyes land on the skyscraper of gloves.

"Shh, don't complain. Bao will find out." Her eyes point toward the black box-like object near the ceiling.

My throat grows dry.

A security camera.

There are *always* guards watching everything. Bao will know and he'll be ruthless. He's going to kill me.

As if hearing my thoughts, the door slams open. A short, round man with red-glowing eyes storms his way to my table.

THUMPTHUMP.

"Girl, I've had enough of you."

He snatches my wrist and I fly out of my chair, slamming into the ground. He tugs, walking into the darkness as I tumble on the floor. I grip the doorway, pulling myself in the opposite direction but I'm like a fly compared to a lion.

A starved grin spreads on his face. "You'd better not struggle this time or else, there will be *severe* consequences."

As he drags me and I thrash around, Uncle passes by and jumps, his head almost crashing into the ceiling. His skin turns into a bleached cloth and his eyes hollow.

"Sir, let me take her wherever you want," he begs.

"No. I will deal with this personally. Don't interfere."

"Please, sir. You will get tired. I can take her."

"No. If you ask one more time, I will kill her and you."

A dark hole forms in the wall, inky black everywhere.

Nothing to see,
Nothing to hear,
Nothing to smell

And nothing to touch.

Only black void.

Until the hands come in.

They aimlessly reach out, the ropes wrapping around me like hungry snakes. The snakes bite into my wrists and shoot out into the darkness in opposite directions. They pull, my arms tearing out as they painfully cross each other.

A grayish shine laughs before my eyes. My ribs crack as my heart pounds against them. An icy chill spreads throughout my body and the air freezes in my lungs.

Snip. Snip.

A soft fluff tickles my feet. I rub it, trying to figure out what it is as more fluffs rain down.

Is it some kind of poisonous cotton?

Deadly silk?

...

It's hair.

My hair.

He's cutting my hair.

A wave of relief washes me. It's better than dying but...my hair was the last piece of culture I have left. The last piece of my former life.

And Bao is taking that away.

Like he's taken everything else.

The icy sorrow and warm joy fight inside me.

My hair is going to be sold to someone oceans away but at least I'm alive.

And still surviving.

"Hala, what happened? Why was Bao so mad? I've never seen him like that before," Uncle asks after Bao dumps me in the cell.

"I...accidentally said something about the work," I mutter, my cheeks catching on fire, "I should've been more careful."

He smiles slightly. "Don't overthink it."

"Bao cut my hair as a punishment."

"But that doesn't change who you are inside. Don't let them watch you weaken. Let them take everything because no matter what, you are free. The soul is always free."

We both stifle laughs, knowing that Bao can be anywhere.

"What is going on here?"

Uncle jerks backward and my eyes catch the flash of a smile on a sinister face.

"No...nothing, sir. I came to make sure she doesn't cause too much noise while crying."

"And why would she be crying?"

"She was upset about her hair but it's nothing, sir."

"Hmm, her hair?"

"Yes, sir. She is a child and you know how children are. They cry at the smallest things."

"Ha, not these children. How old are you, child?"

"I'm thirteen, sir."

"She is *not* a child, Shan. A child is supposed to be under the age of four. Don't make excuses for these dirty workers."

"I'm sorry, sir."

"Now, *Xíngshì*, I need you for a certain task."

A deep, sickening feeling rises from the pit of my stomach. Bao struts out, his booming, aggressive steps tightening the knots in my gut. Uncle freezes there, his eyes drilling into Bao's back. He continues staring,

And staring,

And staring,

until the volcano erupts.

"Don't stare at me like that, *Móguǐ*."

"I..."

"Don't you dare apologize."

The door cracks open and light floods the room, blinding my eyes. The sound of chatting rings in my ears. As my eyes adjust to the light, my insides scream out, begging to be taken away.

25

YIGIRME BESH

BAO IS MAKING me take an interview.

An interview.

My feet grow roots and plant themselves at the doorway. My eyes follow the people moving back and forth, smiles glowing on their faces. A smile begins to grow on my face just before the light

v a n i s h e s

and darkness arrives. An iron hand tears those roots and turns me around to look into the fiery eyes.

"These people want to know what is going on in these buildings. They are going to ask you a few questions and your answers should follow a few *rules.* You're a smart girl but I'm going to remind you of what they are," I nod vigorously, "Good. Number one, you must *never* tell what is going on here and number two, you must praise the Chinese, understand?"

The boulder reappears in my throat. "Yes, master."

"Now, go but remember, I'm *always* watching. If you say anything out of place, you will be punished until my heart is satisfied."

"Yes, master."

The white finally floods in. The bustle of these peculiar people, their giggles, lights a new kind of light inside me. A warm, bright light, not the red, scalding light.

A tall lady in navy blue points at me and everyone clammers around as she walks up. Her white skin shines and her sharp eyes examine everything. Her thin, pink lips softly giggle as a man with a camera says something in gibberish.

"Hello there, my name is Amy and I'm an international reporter. I was born in China but now, I live in the US. What's your name?"

The words turn into dust in my mouth and only a soft croak escapes.

"No need to be shy," she smiles, "Let's try that again. What's your name?"

"An," I mumble, feeling Bao's eyes drilling into my back.

"What a beautiful name. What does it mean?"

"Peace."

"A beautiful name for a beautiful girl. How old are you, An?"

"Thirteen."

"What us adults would give to be thirteen again. Unfortunately, childhood only lasts for a little and then, we're adults with countless responsibilities. Now, An, I will ask you a few questions and I want you to give the most honest and sincere answers you can ever give."

I nod.

I can only give the "honest" responses Bao wants me to give.

"What would you call these buildings?"

"Factories."

"What do you make in these *factories?"*

"Clothes."

"What type of clothes?"

"Gloves, shirts, pants, socks, anything."

"Are you paid?"

"Yes."

"How much?"

"A decent amount."

"How much?"

"Ten *kuai."*

"An hour?"

People are paid by hours? "I'm not sure. I'm not legally old enough to get the money so the boss gives it to my uncle, who stores it."

"So you're not given the money in your own hands?"

"I'm not...but my uncle shows it to me."

Amy's eyes meet Bao's and her smile hardens. "How are the working conditions here?"

"Excellent. The Han Chinese give us all the food and shelter we need. We wouldn't be successful without them."

"The government doesn't do anything...wrong to you, do they?"

"No."

"Do you mind explaining that bruise?"

"What bru..."

Amy points to my wrist. A huge splash of purple, blue and green paints my skin.

I thought I had covered it.

"Oh, it's nothing. I hurt myself."

"You got that big of a bruise from accidentally hurting yourself?"

"I got my hand stuck in a machine. It happens frequently."

"Uh huh."

"The Chinese provide us with opportunities we otherwise wouldn't have had. Without them, we wouldn't be adapting to the changing, advancing world."

"What do the instructors here teach you in order for you to 'adapt' to the ever-changing world," Amy asks, a hint of steel woven into her voice.

"They teach us Mandarin, traditional customs, technology, math, science, everything everyone else around the world is taught. This place is like a boarding school, but for all ages and we also get paid."

Her eyes dart from me, then to Bao and back. "That is all I have for today. If you have anything else to say, contact me. Here is my card. You should have access to a phone or computer, right?"

She hands me a small card with gibberish written on it. By the time I look up, she's gone, talking with a wave of people.

I turn around, heading back into the darkness. At least that's over.

Crash.

My hands fly to my throbbing nose. I don't remember a wall ever being there. As everything stops wobbling in front of me, red and yellow devilish eyes stare right into me. I jerk backward, right before a rigid hand snatches my arm.

"What. Were. You. Thinking?"

26

YIGIRME ALTE

"I DIDN'T DO anything wrong."

"Yes, you did. That lady knows you were lying. You *looked* like you were hiding something. *Guards. Take her."*

Bulky hands grab onto me.

"I did everything you asked me to."

"Tell that to *them,"* Bao booms.

"Stop. *Let me go.* This isn't right."

My words turn into dust. The soldiers drag me, my feet fumbling, closer and closer to the black.

Krik.

A match drowns into a fire and it explodes, melting everything in its path. It burns my arms and legs, fueling them with a newfound strength.

The next few seconds are a blur.

I just remember the struggle.

Guards swarming around me.

Bao's face.

His fear-stricken face.

I remember my fists, clenched in wrath, punching him.

I remember him backing up and begging the guards, begging for Uncle.

I remember Uncle rushing into the hallway to lay eyes upon my brutality and freezing.

I remember charging at him.

I remember the flood of guards swarming around me.

I remember something wet, something cold hitting my face and the darkness.

LIFE GUSHES INTO me like a fresh, cool spring. It spreads throughout my entire body and a tingling feeling comes from my stomach. Two deep, pink, burnt scratches. It looks like someone stapled me there and pulled it out. I touch it and the tingling feeling increases. It's as if someone...tased me.

A faint memory arises. There was a dark, metallic object in Bao's hand, right before I lost consciousness. He must have tased me.

I toss my legs over...the bed?

Since when has Bao given us beds, even if they are terrible quality and deserve to go in the trash?

I stretch my legs, only to touch the opposite wall.

Cling.

My eyes find the handcuff, chaining me to the bed. It digs into my skin as I pull on it.

Reality drops onto me.

This is an isolation cell.

And few make it out of here.

Screeeeech.

*"Guīzé: Cóng bù màofàn...*Rules: Never offend a supervisor. Always respect them because the Uyghurs depend on them for survival. The government provides valuable opportunities to the Uyghurs and they deserve gratitude. The Uyghurs have always been under Han Chinese rule and will never be otherwise. They were never their own peop-"

Crash.

The fury in me explodes.

This has been going on for too long. I can't tolerate it anymore. I'm alone, tired and beaten up. Hasn't it been enough already? How much more do they want from me? Why can't he kill me already?

I glare at the huge padlock on the door,
At the iron bars on the window
And then at the fallen stars of the white plate,
Scattered all over the stone ground.
Screeeeeeech.

"The Uyghurs have always been under Han Chinese rule and will never be otherwise. They were never their own people. They will become civilized only under the guidance and teaching of the Han. If left to their own ways, they will remain stuck in the past and will resort to violent acts to maintain their version of the 'real' world. That is why they are in these re-education camps. They are here to be taught Mandarin, the proper language and other traditional Han customs and history. They are taught how to work and live like other humans rather than remain isolated in their own culture. However, there are rules. If the Uyghurs fail to..."

I try so hard,
So hard,
To block the noise out.
But it's not working.
That cunning,
cruel
Monster.
Screeeeeeeeech.
"Don't ever think about being *smart* again."

Screech.

"If they fail to follow these rules, the punishment will be..."

My hands jump onto my ears again. The handcuff rattles and tugs on my wrist, sinking deeper and deeper. I collapse onto the bed, trying to block out the words but the muffled audio continues ringing in my ears.

"The government is providing Uyghurs with great opportunities to become civilized, like Han Chinese."

I press harder and harder,

as the speech grows louder and louder,

shaking the room like an earthquake.

Come on, you've never given up before, so why now?

The frustration builds up as I bury my head in the flat pillow and thin blanket. The ranting rings in my ears.

The constant chatter of the robotic voice repeating its lies intrudes my dreams, thoughts, everything,

For *days.*

I barely get a few minutes of sleep. Paranoia is waiting on the edge, ready to strike. Red veins crack my eyes, my mind ready to explode.

The hammer pounding,

The drummer beating,

The cymbals crashing.

They all beat my head until I can't feel anything anymore.

I step to the brick wall and *bang*, I bash my head against it.

Bang.

Bang.

Bang.

Bz.

I shoot daggers at the camera, watching my every breath.

My every step.

My every movement.

IT'S BEEN SO many days, I've lost count. The last time I counted, it had been ten days but now, I can't even tell when the day starts and ends. The loneliness has started eating me up and the robotic voice echoes in the room. My body feels so light, I could float right out of the cell through the ceiling. I feel so empty, the rats could burrow into me, building their homes.

Click.

A crisp, cool gush of air rushes in and a flimsy, white tray settles on the ground. I reach out and pull the watery stew and bluish bread toward me, forcing it down my throat. A red blur flashes and my eyes make their way to the thousand-page, red book.

How Communist Rule Helped Xinjiang.

Thud.

"You're going to read that book, young lady. *You don't have a choice."* Bao begins to rant about the benefits of reading the book but his words enter one ear and come out of the other.

I do have the choice whether to read that piece of junk or not.

Thud. Thud.

Click.

The door is thrown open, revealing the stubby man behind it. "It's been two weeks. Have you learned your lesson?"

"Yes, master."

"Good. If you ever misbehave again, there will be worse. I will extract every punishment in my head if you ever do anything like that again."

Click.

The handcuffs slide off my wrist, uncovering the deep, red streaks. I follow him to my usual cell and he shoves me into the ocean of people. I swim my way towards the center and flash the metallic object in my hand. Slight smiles creep on the prisoners' faces and the light in their eyes shines once again.

27

YIGIRME YETTE

"WAKE UP. TIME to get to work," Bao barks once the sun's light barely spreads from the horizon's cracks, "I have a special task for you today. That reporter is back and she wants to speak with you again. *Don't* mess up like last time."

"Yes, master."

I follow Bao through the labyrinth and into a white, glowing room where Amy sits. This time, she is surrounded by emptiness and silence rather than her companions.

"Hello, again. My boss loved your report and told me I have to come back and interview you in more detail.

Here," she glances at Bao and hands me a pad of paper, "Remember, you can tell me anything."

Xiě chū zhenxiàng. Méiyu rén huì zhīdào.

Write the truth. No one will know.

My mouth raises at the corners when I read the printed words on the first page. "I have already told you all you need to know. There is nothing else to the story."

Amy leans in. "There are many countries that don't believe that Uyghurs are going through abuse. Many more countries than those that want to help you. If we want to gain their support, we need your story. We need every bit of information we can get to prove them wrong and to help you all. But that can't happen if you won't tell the truth."

"I've already told you the truth. There *isn't* anything more to tell."

"At least write down what you *told* me last time."

I nod and put the pencil against the paper.

Xiě zhège de shíhòu wo kěnéng huì bèi shā...

It's been a few nights and bullets haven't pierced my heart yet. Uncle's face drains into a grayish-yellowish color. The shadows around his eyes expand and the crimson veins in his eyes spread like little rivers.

The paranoia sets in like a virus attacking. Bao could come anytime. He could be in any corner and shoot me in a split second. He could come and kill me in my sleep.

Thud. Thud.

Heavy, rushed footsteps creep closer and closer and everyone shoots up and freezes like statues.

Crash.

The door throws itself open at the command of the swaying snakes. They slither in but no one fights.

No one screams.

They all cast their eyes down.

In humiliation and shame, despite not having done anything wrong.

"A news article about this factory and the real conditions. Written by that fancy lady. I can't punish her but I can punish you all," his eyes set on me, *"You did this, didn't you? You gave her the details? Guards!"*

"Wait, sir-"

"Do. Not. Interfere. Shan."

"Keep her alive, sir."

"And why should I keep this *slave* alive?"

"Put her on TV and make her deny the report and call it a lie. It would boost the government's reputation."

Bao freezes for a few seconds, swimming in his thoughts.

"That would be better," The tight line on his face curls into a vile smirk, "Prepare the cameras. We're going live."

"MANY OF YOU have read the recent news article by a certain journalist named Amy. The words may seem true but they are not. You have been led to believe in this lie. I am a Uyghur girl in a re-education program and it has completely changed my life. The Chinese government has provided others, like me, with education, healthcare, work and so much more that we alone could not have achieved.

"The Han care. They care about us. They don't want us to be left behind but want us to adapt and become the best versions of ourselves. They have opened a door of opportunity for us so that we can advance as the rest of the world is. In the education programs they offer, we are given free food and shelter. They teach us Mandarin, Han customs and other skills needed to work in the modern world. All of these skills are necessary to survive.

"These blasphemous lies about them are ways to bring China down. The rest of the world is just jealous. They all want China's success. None of us are being forced to work against our will and we are not abused here. This is a place where we are welcomed.

"To summarize, the rumors and slander spreading about China and the so-called "genocide" are simply lies to make the government look bad. China has given us, the Uyghurs, many gifts, among them work and education. They are giving us the tools to survive this harsh world. Thank you."

I spit out the thorny words as they tear my throat and a wave of relief washes me.

It's finally over.

"You did well today. As a reward, I won't kill you."

What an *amazing* reward.

28

YIGIRME SEKKIZ

HE. HEHE.

My heavy eyelids flutter open to the sound of...laughter.

The blurry world grows crisp as if my eyes have been washed. A pair of little, dark eyes gleam in front of me.

Hehe. He.

The smiling baby grips onto me, his legs wobbling as he struggles to stand up. He stumbles and falls onto the rock floor. His toothless grin grows wider, mumbled sounds come out of his mouth.

Brrrru. Annu. Maaaaaaaa.

He claps his hands, gurgles and peers deeply into my eyes.

Aa.

He clutches my finger and pulls, playing with it and putting it in his mouth. A smile spreads onto my face. The other prisoners rise, their eyes resting on the child in front of me.

Thud. Thud.

A bullet of panic shoots through my heart. I throw him to the person next to me, who hands him to his mother.

"Where is it," Bao bellows.

ThumpThump.

"Where. Is. It?"

THUMPTHUMP.

"Where. Is. It?"

Silence.

I glance sideways at the woman clutching her baby, holding him as if he's melting away.

Creeak.

"I guess I'll have to find it myself."

Bao swims through the hollow-eyed workers, his eyes hungrily searching for its prey. They come to rest on the woman and her child. The greed and cruelty dance in his eyes. He tears the baby from his mother.

Raaaaa. Raaaa.

The child screams and cries as Bao examines him, the piercing sounds tearing my ears.

"You thought I wouldn't find out about this dog? You thought you could hide him for months on end and I wouldn't know about it? *You were wrong.* I'm *always watching.* This animal is too loud. It can't be here. Next time, have a mute baby." He swims towards the door, the shrieking baby squirming and kicking in his arms.

"Take me instead. Please. Don't take him. He's just a baby. He hasn't done anything. Please. *Please. Please,"* the woman pleads as Bao disappears behind the impenetrable walls, the baby's screams still echoing until a deafening, sickening silence floats in.

A few prisoners wrap the woman in their arms, trying to comfort the tear-stricken mother. Her bloodshot eyes leak tears until there aren't any more left.

"Omar didn't deserve to die. He didn't deserve to die. He didn't deserve to die. Bao should have taken me instead."

The rest of us force ourselves out of the cell.

"You, you and *you,"* Bao makes his way towards me and two other workers, "are going to have different jobs."

We follow him into a smokey building. My eyes bulge out of their sockets as I count each piece of dirty, soot-covered machine. Dim, scattered light gleams off the chunks of metal.

"You are going to fill in for some useless workers until I find replacements. Now, get to work."

A COAT OF crimson is painted over my hands and arms and splotches of blue and purple are stuck onto me. Pain throbs throughout my limbs as the air struggles to fit inside my lungs.

It's been a month since I was separated from my brother. It's been a month since I've been living in this

Killing

Field.

"And you'll never ever leave..." Bao's voice cackles inside my throbbing head.

Eeeeeeeeeeee.

All the workers drop what they are doing and flock into a room in front of the factory and rush into the dark, barren room, sweeping me with them. Everyone sits on the floor, facing a tall, boney figure.

What is this place?

"All right, class. Where did we leave off?"

The zippers on everyone's mouths remain closed.

"No one is going to answer? Don't you Uyghurs have brains? We left off on page one hundred thirty-nine. Open your books to page one hundred forty."

Everyone flips through the thousand-page book. I peer into my neighbor's book, not wanting to stand out.

"You, start reading," the woman commands. The prisoner begins muttering in a dull, shaky voice.

"After the Communist party took control of the power in China, the nation has soared above all others. The just rulings of the current president, Xi Jinping, have granted many people new jobs and have boosted China's economy, making it a global power. However, he doesn't only focus on the economy, he also focuses on the people. Xi Jinping has a dream to give all people a chance to live better lives, including the Uyghurs. He believes that after going through 're-education,' the Uyghurs will rise to be like the ethnic Han Chinese. However, this will only happen if the Uyghurs listen and accept the change that's good for them. Some of them are naturally rebellious and malicious so the government is going to have to get rid of them for the benefit of society."

"Enough. Now you read."

The next person recites in the same tone as the first.

EEEEEEEEEEEE.

Everyone swarms out of the classroom, the *buzzz* of the hopeless voices still ringing in their ears.

"Please."

"You can't. You will be going against the rules," the woman answers.

"Please. Only for a few seconds. I haven't looked at the sky in months," the man begs.

"I can't let you."

"Please. Just one second."

The woman's eyes meet the guard's and the man disappears into the darkness, his cries silenced. Not a single eye looks in his direction. All remain glued to the floor.

"Hurry up. You all have another lesson," the teacher orders.

Everyone files through a door into an enormous, dark room. A white sheet on a stage lights up and a picture of a slightly smiling face appears. His black suit and the red flag behind him give it all away. Xi Jinping stares at us, his prominent eyes and wrinkled face plastered onto the screen.

Creeeeee.

A sharp, scratchy sound echoes throughout the room.

"Good afternoon. As you all know, I am Bao, this facility's supervisor. Can anyone tell me who the displayed man is?"

"Xi Jinping," the chorus responds.

"Great job. Maybe you all aren't as barbaric as I thought you are. This legendary man is the president of China. He has provided all of us, Han and Uyghur, the opportunities to change our lives for the better. He has given you all the resources to learn the proper Han Chinese way.

Unfortunately, not all of you have adapted to this way of life. Therefore, it is my responsibility to guide you all to the right path by starting with the topic of religion. You *Yěmán rén* believe in Islam, a fanatic, false religion. The first step to assimilating to Han culture is to denounce this dangerous religion.

We all agree *animals* don't live properly, right? We all want to help them but they continue doing what they want to do. They attack and kill people for no reason. That's what you all are. The government is trying to help you but you insist on being *misguided.*

Xi Jinping wants to help you become like the rest of us. He wants to protect China from you because you are dangerous. You have never loved China and want it to fall. We can't allow that, can we? We need to keep China flourishing and that will only be achieved once you dogs are all imprisoned, dead or assimilated into Chinese culture. You inflicted this suffering upon yourselves. You are animals and continue to breed animals. You all are the only obstacle China has until it experiences full glory."

This goes on for hours and hours. My mind wanders from place to place as Bao's voice buzzes on and on. He likes hearing his own voice. Guards circle around us, their rifles loaded.

"This question will test whether you love your country or not. Does. Allah. Exist?"

"No," everyone replies, their eyes cast downward. A few sparkling beads drip down and *cli,* echo throughout the whole room.

Everyone says no except me.

The words lodge in my throat, unable to come out.

"All of you passed the test. All of you but one. Guards."

The soldiers swarm towards me, their arms wrapping around me like a rope. A sharp, blinding, metallic shine comes from above and

Thwack.

Thwack.

Thwack.

Thick, iron-like objects crack my bones. Tiny streams course down my face and drip onto the ground. The rifles smashing into me are coated with the crimson that has painted my surroundings. The glimmering darkens with each *thwack.*

"Enough," Bao booms, "Obey those superior to you, especially if you want to become civilized. Next time, it will be *much, much worse."*

"Yes, master," I croak, pain shooting through every bone.

As the moon climbs the stars, my work begins anew. Despite the crusted red all over me, I stand in front of the glaring crowd. There is now double the amount of space in the cell with a few people leaving almost every night.

"38 and 43, it's time for you to go. You know the procedure. Hurry before Bao comes."

"Too late."

29

YIGIRME TOQQUZ

CRACK.

Kraaaak.

The little rectangle of light disappears, black taking its place. It circles around, exploring its new victim. It pokes and stabs as I swim through the black hole, searching for the tiniest speck of light. My entire body fades away with each step.

Creeeeeeeeak.

A flash of white blinds me like a thousand suns ambushing me.

Thud. Thud.

Aggressive footsteps echo in the room, singing with my panicked heart. My blood turns to ice and my feet plant themselves in the ground. A fuzzy, dark figure clouds my vision.

"Shan. Come in here at *once."*

Thud.

Thud.

Thud.

Thud.

Thud.

Uncle's jaw falls slightly and his eyes hollow out. The slight tremor in his hand rings like a drum. His feet dig themselves into the ground and I watch as Uncle turns into a stone statue with surprise glued to his face.

"Do you know her?"

Deafening silence.

"Do. You. Know. Her?"

"No."

"Do not lie to me, Shan. If you don't tell me right now, I will kill both of you. Answer me, Núlì."

"Y...Y...Ye...Y...es."

"Who is she? T*ell me this instant."*

"A prisoner."

"Do not lie to me."

"She's a prisoner."

"Shan."

"She's a prisoner..."

"And?"

"M...M...My niece."

"That's why you show compassion towards her. You know what, Shan? I will be merciful to you like you were to this girl. You have been at my side for a while now. It's as if you've been my loyal assistant forever," a greedy, smug grin spreads on Bao's face.

Uncle's eyes light up, a lone tear streaming down his cheek.

"Kill her."

"What?" Uncle and I both blurt.

"Kill her."

"You tyrant. You vile monster," the words slip.

"What. Did. You. Say?"

The bubble bursts inside. "You heard me."

"Do you realize who you're talking to, you little *Mogui?"*

Uncle's eyes beg me.

No, he mouths but all I can feel is the red-hot lava. "I'm talking to a *person.* A human being."

"You clever girl. You have no idea what I can do to you. No idea. That little mercy I had for you is now dried up. I will have fun with you. I will make you experience every *single* punishment I can think of."

"Please, sir-"

"Shan. And in the end, your beloved uncle will be the one who enjoys it the most. He will be the one to take your life away."

"She's just a child," Uncle pleads.

"She isn't *anymore*. She's a dirty traitor, a *Xíngshì*. Do you understand? Don't ask for mercy again."

Uncle opens and closes his mouth, the words freezing. A lone tear streams down his cheek, leaving a wet river behind. The roots holding my feet down loosen. Each step is painful and the tangled roots tear at my feet as I take a step towards Uncle.

Crack. Crack. Crack.

The world goes black for a few seconds. Flashes of pain throb all over and my heart beats in my head. The light rushes back in, revealing Bao with the thick, long, bloodstained stick in his hands.

"Don't."

Thwack.

"You."

Thwack.

"Dare."

Thwack.

"Go."

Thwack.

"To."

Thwack.

"Him."

MY HEAVY EYELIDS open up to pitch-black. It's as if I'm in outer space, where there is no light and no sign of life. I try lifting my hands but something holds them down. I try the same with my feet, with no luck. I thrash around in the restraints until a blinding light burns my eyes.

"It's no use. You can't escape. Do you know what this machine is? It's a water-boarder. I'm sure a *child* like you has never heard of such a thing. Isn't that what your uncle calls you? Well, let me tell you its purpose. It will dunk you in the water repeatedly until...you admit your mistake. Start it."

Whzzzzz.

Clung.

The icy water bites at my face and the air fights inside my lungs. It scratches and claws for hours until I surface up.

Clung.

Clung.

Clung.

My brain wobbles violently in my skull after going

Up and down.

Up and down.

Up and down.

"This is getting boring. Too repetitive. I have something else in mind for you. Don't worry, it will be even more fun," Bao chuckles.

I don't struggle when the guards take me to another room.

I don't struggle when they force me to sit on a wooden chair.

I don't struggle when they strap my wrists and ankles and when they attach wires.

Because my energy is gone.

And so has the little speck of hope I had left.

Bzzzz.

Bzzzzzz.

Bzzzzzzzzzzz.

The white-hot pain surges through my body, rattling it like a toy. I tremble violently, the electricity coursing through, lighting me on fire. A foul, smoky smell rises everywhere. The thick, black air stings my eyes and a new pain arises.

It's as if something is eating my hand.

I peer down to see the orange chewing my hand.

"Fire. Fire. Fire."

Splash.

I rub the water from my eyes. My hand cools down but the crumpled, black flesh remains. The ropes slip off and the color returns to the room.

"Do you realize how expensive that is?"

"It's not my fault it caught on fire."

"Whose fault is it then?"

"The person who was operating it and especially the person who started this whole thing."

"I'm finished with you. You have caused me a few thousand kuai. Shan."

"Yes, sir."

"Get rid of her this instant."

"Bu...but-"

"Don't argue."

"Please, sir-"

"I guess I'll just have to do it myself."

Click.

I wait,

And wait,

And wait,

But nothing happens.

Not a single peep comes from Bao or Uncle.

"Shan, get your dirty hands off me."

Uncle's hand rests on a now red Bao's shoulder.

"Shan, *now."*

"No."

"What did you say?"

"You can't kill her. I'm tired of being treated like this."

"Ah, it seems like you've forgotten what I could do. If I wanted to, I could do much more to her and you. You wouldn't want that, would you," Uncle's eyes hollow and the little courage in them fades away, "Kill her. *Now."*

Uncle stumbles towards me. I back up until the wall hugs me.

"I'm so sorry, Hal...An. I'm so sorry." A tear drips down his face.

Uncle snatches a rope and forms a noose. Before I can blink, the noose grips my neck and squeezes. I clutch it and try to force it down but it just bites harder.

THUMPTHUMP.

THUMPTHUMP.

THUMPTHUMP.

My blood freezes and my head throbs.

My lungs beg for air.

As each agonizing second passes, life claws its way out. The darkness swarms in and wraps me in its blanket, its glowing eyes slowly

F

A

D

I

N

G

away.

ÜRKESH

THE NEXT DAY

30

OTUZ

THE FAINT LIGHT tickles my face, forcing my eyelids to crack open. It paints my surroundings with gray and black, the menacing shadows creeping closer and closer. I turn onto my back, the iron floor hugging me. Shocks of fiery pain light me up, each part of me catching on fire.

"You're finally awake," a scratchy, squeaky voice booms.

I lift my head, locking eyes with the short, stocky man.

"If you hadn't woken up, that would be a very different problem. Or actually, it would be the solution to the problem."

"You're not Chen..." I sputter, the words barely forming.

"No, I'm not. I'm Bao, the camp supervisor. Chen is a good friend of mine. He wanted to get rid of a *certain* prisoner so he sent that prisoner over here. Now, I'm a civilized man. I don't want to kill you so if you *behave*, I'll let you go. If you don't, you know what will happen," a sick, slow smile crawls on his face, "Enough of that. Get to work."

My eyes beg to close once more and my limbs glue themselves to the floor. It takes all my energy to force my throbbing head off the ground. I lift my sore back and my dead legs, fighting the force pulling me back down. The little seed of hope I had has drowned in waves of despair, buried in a sea of grief.

Drip. Drip.

This place isn't any different from Chen's camp.

It's the same blackness, the same emptiness.

The same screams and the same cursing echoes.

The same angry stomping and the same beating.

Creeeeeeeak.

The same buzz of workers.

The same empty, hopeless, weeping faces.

The same towering machinery, the same tasks.

The same scowl on each guard's face.

It's as if I'd never been deported to another camp.

It's as if I can still see Chen barking orders.

It's all the same.

The same tears.

The same fear.

The same silence.

Only a different, equally brutal supervisor.

I'm still one among an ocean of workers, a stranger, a ghost. The hollow faces float around like ghosts. But one particular ghost terrorizes me the most. My feet bury into the floor and my blood turns into ice.

The pale, drained, wet face of my uncle.

The bush of thick, black hair is now gone and the former rough expression has evaporated. A weak, weeping man is left. Black circles shadow his eyes and only the bones are left on his body.

But he's still my uncle.

My feet propel forward, moving at the speed of light until I'm face-to-face with the man.

"Uncle?"

He looks up, searching deep into my eyes. The tears drip faster and faster with each minute until he's a sobbing mess.

"I'm broken, Ürkesh. I'm broken."

"You can fix it."

"I can't. It's too late. It can't be fixed anymore."

"At least get back to work."

"I can't."

"Why?"

"Because he's not a worker," Bao interrupts, "He's my assistant. He helps me."

I cast my eyes down, pretending as if I never heard the words ring in my ears.

"Didn't you hear me, *Gǒu*?"

"I'm sorry, sir."

"Don't ca-That's right. You're new here. There are two rules here. Do you know what they are?"

"No, sir."

"Number One: *Always* obey me. Number Two: Call me master."

"What?"

"Didn't you hear what I said a few seconds ago?"

"I'm sorry, si...master."

"I'll let it slide but only because you're new here. Next time, there will be consequences. Now, get to work."

I squish into an empty space next to a machine. It snorts and grunts nonstop like an angry bull. Images of Uncle sobbing play again and again in my head, a spark of fear lighting each time. Bao's words ring in my ears.

Assistant.

Assistant.

Assistant.

They haunt me as I work.

They haunt me as I close my eyes.

They stalk me for hours until my brain shuts down and the night closes in.

"HURRY UP. I don't have a hundred years for you slaves to get up."

We all jump up and rush to the "cafeteria," more like another dungeon. We stuff the rotten piece of bread and the black water down our throats and fly to the factory. Our hands move like robots but our minds soar to the sky.

All except mine.

Mine buries itself into a grave, thinking about Uncle, all while keeping an eye on Bao. The second he disappears behind a restricted door, I creep towards Uncle.

"Uncle, I have a question. Why were you crying like that yesterday?"

His eyes hollow and tears begin climbing up, barely containing themselves.

“Why are you crying?”

Uncle shakes his head.

“Uncle, tell me what’s wrong.”

"Hala."

31

OTUZ BIR

"HALA WAS...HERE?"

"For a few months."

"Where is she now?"

A tear streams down his cheek, leaving a wet river in its place. "She's gone."

"Where? Where did she go?"

Another tear.

And another.

And another.

"She's in Heaven, *Háizi.*"

The words echo in my ears.

Hala's gone.

Hala's gone.

Hala's gone.

Everything's gone. Mama and Papa are gone. Yu is gone. Hala is gone. My sister, who I never cared about, is gone. I will never, ever see my family again. I will never be able to escape with them.

I'm...alone.

My heart shatters and the tears blur my vision.

"H...How?"

"Bao killed her."

"How?"

"She was strangled."

"How? Why?"

"Bao made me."

"Bao made you what? What did he make you do?"

"He made me...strangle her."

"You did what?"

"Ürkesh, quiet down. Bao will hear you. He'll kill you too."

"You. Did. What?"

"He made me strangle her."

"Why did you do it?"

"I'm a coward. I tried to resist but I couldn't."

Now the tears are pouring out.

"It's not really Uncle's fault for all this. It's Bao's," The Voice remarks.

You're right.

"Stop crying, Uncle. It wasn't your fault. At least she's in a better place now."

"Now she doesn't have to suffer," he whispers, the dripping slowing down.

"Get up and do something. We have to get out of this place before it's too late."

"Not now, Ürkesh. Not now."

I nod cautiously and go back to work.

SHHHHHHOOOOO.

Drenched air sleeps in the room.

Sccrrrrr.

The moldy brush glides on the toilet's surface as I try to scrub off the fungus and dirt. Green and pink splotches paint the exterior and it reeks like rotten socks.

Creeeeak.

Heavy footsteps walk up the slippery hallway and a stout figure appears from the shadows. A flash of greed lights up in his eyes. His hands reach behind him and grip a clear bottle, filled with a yellowish-green liquid. He places it behind the shower curtain. A few seconds later, a tiny hand reaches out and grabs the bottle.

Aaaaaah.

Aaaaaaaaaaah.

AAAAAAAAAAAAAAAAAAAAAAAAAAH.

The piercing, bloodcurdling screams echo throughout the room, sending bullets of panic through my heart. The calming splatter of water ceases and a girl steps out of the shower, her clothes soaking and sticking onto her skin. Angry, puffy patches of red are splotched all over her body and her eyes are lifeless and cloudy. Raw, red skin is what remains on her face. I grab my bucket of water and dump it on her. I dab a damp cloth on her eyes, but they remain the same: foggy and hollow.

"I can't see," she whispers.

"Where are your parents?"

"Will I ever see again?"

"I don't know. I don't know."

The heavy breathing of the person beside me drives the sleep out of me. I turn around to face the wall and massage my sore back. Memories play in front of my eyes and I reach out to touch my family but they fade away and instead, a cold surface greets my hand. The damp, dark wall comes into sight and the world begins to spin as my heavy eyes close.

Fog runs around, everything turning into white. Biting wind chews at my bones as my teeth rattle together. The ground is a dull brown, with not a single plant blooming. Nothing but white greets me. I squint as a slightly dark patch of white catches my eyes. The form has the shadow of a...human.

"Hello? Hello?" I reach out to touch the man but when my fingers brush against his shirt, he crumples to the ground.

"Are you okay?"

I turn him over.

Everything stops.

My eyes are glued to his face.

My hand jerks backward as air is rapidly pumped in and out of my lungs. A blizzard freezes my back and my blood erupts in my veins.

Splotches of red flesh are painted on his face but the rest is bones. Ivory, shining bones. His glass-like eyes are fixed on the sky.

When I finally tear my eyes off, other figures are sprawled on the ground. I run to every one of them, turning them over.

But all of them are in the same condition as the first.

A hand grips my shoulder.

My body freezes.

My heart pounds against my ribs.

I turn over to look into Chen's eyes.

His wild, merciless, blazing eyes.

His disheveled hair spikes up like thorns and crimson paints his clothes. His sharp teeth flash like death right before it strikes.

A white glimmer shoots from his hand.

"Oh, I'll have fun with you like the others. This time, you won't be able to escape me."

My heart climbs to my throat, not a single sound escaping from it before *sloosh*, my vision turns red.

Huuuuuaaaah.

A sharp sting jolts me out of my sleep. My ankles and wrists are bound to a chair and sticky, paper-like objects are stuck everywhere.

Bzzzzz.

Aaaaah.

A short man appears in the darkness. "Please, master. I haven't done anything wrong."

"You're a Uyghur. That's the problem. And also, you helped that girl. You know who that's against the rules."

"I...I...I can't control the fact that I'm Uyghur."

"Have you ever thought about not being born?"

"I can't control that."

"Isn't being a *Zuìfàn* your fault?"

"I'm not a criminal. None of us are. Our religion advocates for peace, not violence."

"No, it doesn't. You all are our enemies. You're a threat to the stability of China. I can't let you go free without calming that inner rebelliousness of yours. You also went against my orders. I never told you to help the girl but you did anyway."

"I'm sorry, master. I didn't know. You can let me go. I promise I won't tell anyone what happens here. No one will know."

"What are you going to tell everyone?"

"I'll come up with something."

"Like what?"

"I'll tell them I got lost in the forest and couldn't find my way back."

"You got lost in a forest for a few months. And you expect them to believe you?"

"It's happened before. They'll believe me."

"Hmm...I'll think about it. Nevermind, I know the answer. Ye-No."

"No?"

"No."

"But-"

"It is my job to protect China and its people from threats like you. Would you let a criminal go if you ever caught him? No, you wouldn't. Same thing here. I can't let you go. It's like letting a murderer go after he has killed ten people."

"Please, master. I'm not a murderer or a criminal. I haven't done anything wrong to anyone. I'm just a kid."

"You aren't a kid anymore. You're about seventeen, not six."

"Please."

"Stop that annoying little mouth of yours." Bao disappears behind the thick, towering door.

Bzzzzz.

Bzzzzzzz.

Bzzzzzzzzzzz.

MY EYES flutter open, the black greeting me.

"Good, you're awake. I was getting bored." Bao nods slightly at the guards, who stand me up.

"Sit, my child. I'm sure you're tired."

A guard shoves me into the chair.

Eeeeiiiiii.

"Please. Please."

Thousands of nails fish into my flesh, gluing me to the chair. The slightest movement sends them digging deeper and deeper. White-hot pain flashes across my whole body as if electricity is streaming through me. A wet red stream drips onto the floor, its drips echoing throughout the room.

"Child, you're sitting in a chair. It's not like you're in pain or anything."

"Please, make it stop."

"GET UP, *NÚLÌ.*"

I crack open my eyelids a little.

"Get up."

I force my eyes open to see myself drowning in a lake of crimson. Pain rips through me as I roll out. Burnt, flaked skin dots my arms and legs as bloody, pink, angry patches of flesh are painted all over. The place where the protective, pink shells were on my fingers are torn off, swollen skin taking its place.

I clutch my throbbing head and lift myself off the ground. A searing hot ache throws me off balance. Before I tumble to the floor, a bulky hand grips my arm.

"Here, this will help." Bao hands me a white pill.

"Don't take it. It's the same pill Chen gave you," The Voice warns.

"It's okay, master. I'm fine."

"You don't *look* fine. Come on, take it. It will make you feel better."

"Thank you, sir-I mean master." I snatch the pill and swallow it whole.

A weird sound escapes my lips a minute later. A hysterical giggle, then full-on laughter. I clutch my stomach and fall to the ground, laughing so hard that tears are streaming out of my eyes. Then, I feel empty. It feels like I'm floating.

"I told you not to take it," Bao scolds mockingly.

"Stoouuup. It's not like me had a choice. You foooooced in down me troat."

"Why did you do this? Now, we have one less worker," a deep, heavy voice squeaks.

"Don't talk to me like that, Shan. I'm your supervisor. Besides, it's temporary. It will wear off the effects."

"Effects of what?"

"The electric shock."

"You electrocuted him?"

"Shan, watch who you're talking to. I shouldn't have to remind you so many times to respect those superior to you."

"I'm sorry, master."

"You'd better be. Now, what is this place? A hotel? No. It is a re-education camp to help you all. I can't help you if his rebellious tendencies display themselves. Don't tell me what to do, *Yěmán rén."*

Uncle nods silently, his glum eyes glancing at me every minute.

"I'm fuune, Uncli."

My mind goes blank and I lose complete control over my body. A blanket of black wraps around me, its warmth comforting me.

Grrrrr.

A deep pain jolts me out of my sleep. My stomach. The growling beast unleashes its anger onto my insides, tearing it. I stand up, trying to distract myself when I see it.

"Chen told me you had experience with this. It's delicious actually. Tender, juicy meat with a spicy drink. Mmmmm. You'll like it," Bao remarks.

My heart pounds against my ribcage, slowly cracking it open. My breathing gets heavier and heavier as I glare at the plate.

"You don't have a choice. You have to eat it."

"Please, I can't."

"Yes, you can."

"Please."

"You'd better eat that or else your time is up, boy."

I tear a piece of the pork off and shove it down my throat.

"Don't show Bao your tears. It will only make him feel satisfied," The Voice gently says.

I don't listen and begin quietly sobbing. An arrogant smirk spreads on Bao's face. "Once you're done, you can go to the bathroom but only if you finish the whole plate."

The food and wine climb up my throat and collect in my mouth.

Don't throw up. Don't throw up.

I swallow the bitter vomit and drag myself to the bathroom, clutching my stomach. Every minute, the line creeps closer and closer to the door until it's my turn. The door slams shut and the smell of waste and mold slaps my nose. Within a split second, all the pork and wine are in the toilet.

Bz.

I peer up and my eyes land on the camera glaring at me.

"Time's up." A shadow darkens the mini-room and a pair of hands throw me outside. "Next time, get done faster. Now, get to work," the squeaky voice warns.

"Yes, sir," I croak, the taste of vomit still lingering in my mouth. I push open the factory doors and jump into the sea of people. Right before I'm swept away, a hand jolts me backward.

"You took a long time in the bathroom today. What were you doing in there?" Bao interrogates.

"I went to the bathroom, master."

"That's not the correct answer. I'm asking you what you did in the bathroom. The cameras show that you were trying to escape by breaking through the wall." A slim, sly smile creeps on his face.

"That's not what I was doing, master."

"Then, what were you doing?"

"I was doing what people do in the bathroom."

"Don't be clever with me. *What. Were. You. Doing?"*

"I was...throwing up."

"You vomited the food I graciously provided you? Tsk, tsk. This is unacceptable. Guards."

"Please, *master."*

"Raising your voice in front of your superior. Even more unacceptable."

Iron wraps around my arms and jerks me backward, my legs flying.

"Mercy, master, mercy."

"You've made too many unforgivable mistakes. I can't let them go now," He looks towards his soldiers, "You may have fun with him."

Fliop.

A black covering wraps around my face, the air growing heavier each second. The ground disappears from under my feet.

Crash.

I tumble into a tight object.

Slllll.

From above, something covers the object.

Crash. Thud. Krrrrrrr.

The world spins violently, my whole body jerking fiercely.

Kroom. Krra. Thud.

The world spins faster and faster, my head spinning with it. My brain wobbles inside my skull, colliding with it. My limbs are cramped and contorted, all wrapped around each other.

Then it stops.

Silence.

Slllll.

Clllla.

The ground falls out from under my feet.

Crash.

Thwack.

Crack.

The bees sting from everywhere, my flesh burning.

Krrrr.

Wheppp.

Sllllll.

Thwack..

Thwack.

Thwack.

THE PAIN SHOOTS through me, jerking me out of my "coma."

"*Móguǐ,* help Shan with his job. The *Bèndàn* isn't in his proper senses," a voice commands, not caring that I'm colored red and purple.

"Yes, master."

Bao shoos me away and puts his ear to his phone. "Yes?"

Hushed, distant murmurs come from the phone. "I'm dealing with him. You sent him here for me to take care of so stop calling me every minute. You know I'm doing what you asked so please, stop calling me when I'm working."

More murmurs.

"Not literally. Anyway, I have a job to get to. Bye."

The instant he turns back, I'm swimming in the ocean of people.

What was that all about? Am I the 'him' he was referring to?

"Of course you are. He's planning to kill you. You need to get out as soon as possible," The Voice says.

A tall, skeletony figure clouds my eyes. "Bao sent me to help you."

"What. Happened?" Uncle asks, a hint of worry hidden in his voice once the light shines on me.

"The...usual...I have something to tell you though. Bao was talking to someone on the phone and he mentioned a certain 'him' he wants to get rid of. I think he was referring to...me. It's been two weeks since I've been here and I'm afraid I don't have much more time. We need to escape."

"*You* need to escape," Uncle mutters, "But I...I can't. It's too risky. I can help you though. Do you have a plan?"

"I don't know anything about this camp."

"I can help with that. When Hala...was here, she would help others escape. At the time, Bao had a killing fever. But then, she was caught," his eyes glisten, "I know some places from which she used to get out of the camp without being seen. But first, you're going to need food and supplies."

"*This* is the food. Why is there so much? What is it doing here?"

"Shhh. Bao keeps it here as psychological torture for me. Now, put as much as you can carry."

I stuff the sack with all the colors I can grab. It's like I'm packing a rainbow. Once I'm done, I bury the sack in the rest of the food.

"You have to escape tonight. Bao has a party to attend today so he's letting most of the guards take the night off. There are only going to be ten guards remaining."

"But how will I get out of the cell?"

Uncle flashes a shiny, metal object. "I may have learned some things from your sister," he grins and hands me the key, "Goodbye, Ürkesh."

Uncle pulls me into a tight bear hug as if he's never going to see me again. "Please come with me," I beg.

"I can't. It's too risky. Besides, who's going to help the rest of the prisoners here? I will continue the work Hala started."

"If you ever change your mind..."

"I know," he smiles, a few tears dripping from his eyes as his hand unlatches from my shoulder.

32

OTUZ IKKI

THE CRICKETS SING their mournful songs, hoping the wandering souls are listening. The wind gently hums alongside them, carrying the tune away. The trees reach out to squeeze their prey while the fading moon stares blankly at its realm. The sweet, fresh autumn air tickles my nose and the bleeding red and orange laugh as they embrace the leaf. Dead leaves lay fallen on the ground, slowly fading into nothing.

Crack.

I freeze, my feet gluing themselves to the dirt and my blood turning into ice.

Snap.

My feet begin to fly as the trampled leaves shriek. *It could be a snake, a bear, a wolf, a leopard or...the police.*

My heart races and pounds against my bones, rattling them until they begin cracking. The trees *whoosh* by and the air grows hard and cold, struggling to escape my lungs.

Crack.

I curl into a ball and slam right into the mud, the force of the fall rolling me down the slight slope. I scan the area only to find the same green and brown staring back at me.

Like a sloth, I inch up the incline, the trees getting smaller and smaller every minute. Within a few more minutes, the trees are nothing but dots on the ground.

As the sun begins to rest, the dark, lush green turns into a lighter, calming green as the towering trees become stones on the horizon.

"After you have passed the dense forest of Xinjiang and you reach a lightly wooded area, know that you are on the right path. Continue on until you pass through a desert and reach a road that goes through the Himalayas. Once you reach the border, you are safe. But be careful. There are wild animals everywhere and when Chen finds out, he will become the most dangerous predator."

"How long would the journey take?" I asked him.

"About three to four weeks."

Taio had told me that right before we broke out of Chen's camp. He told me that in case things didn't turn out right.

Tears fill the brim of my eyes. The ghosts of my loved ones eat me from the inside. The loneliness bites at me as each step unlocks a distant memory. Hala's radiant smile spreads across the sun while the wind carries Mama's hum. Papa's deep laughs shake the trees and Yu's jokes make the birds giggle. Taio's deep, calming voice makes the plants radiate.

My legs begin to tremble and my heart grows heavy. I sit under a tree and close my eyes.

Crack.

"Ismail."

I'm back in my house, inside the pitch-black hideout. The thuds upstairs cackle louder each second.

"Please. Please. Please."

"Shut up, *Gǒu*," a heavy voice yells.

"Please, Chen. Please, leave me alone."

"Where is he? *Where. Is. The. Móguǐ?"*

"I don't know who you're talking about."

"You liar. You dirty liar. Don't worry, I'll find him and he will suffer, all because of you."

Thud. Thud. Thud.

The echoing footsteps soon become like gentle hums in the distance. The screaming and begging do too. Soon, they are inaudible and I warp back into reality, beads of sweat streaming down my face. The air grows heavy in my lungs and I claw at it, trying to breathe.

"It was just a dream," The Voice comforts.

A dream? It was a nightmare.

"Dreams and nightmares aren't reality."

But they are terrifying.

"But they're fake."

Chen was in my nightmare. He was the officer upstairs.

"No one knows if that occurred."

But I know it did.

Crack.

I spring off the ground and listen as the grass underneath me shrieks. The plains inch farther and farther as the sun crawls up the sky and back down. The wind tickles the plants and they laugh, the soothing sound flying through the air. The distant screeches of eagles and the muddish, shaggy yak dot the fields, their occasional grunts ringing throughout the land. The sounds synchronize to form a rhythm.

Thud. Screeee. Shhhh.

Thud. Scree. Shhh.

"Our country is a garden.

In the garden, the brightly colored flowers are beautiful.

The warm sunlight is shining on us.

Everyone smiles.

Wa ha ha. Wa ha ha.

Everyone smiles.

Sisters, come here quickly.

Brothers, don't go away.

Hand in hand we will sing a song together.

How happy is our life.

Wa ha ha. Wa ha ha.

How happy is our life."

The words flow out like a river. I hum the tune, again and again, joining the melody of the wind and eagles. A tear drips down my face. Mama used to sing that to me before I went to sleep when I was young.

Slowly, the trees fade away, leaving a barren, dry land. It's been two weeks since I've been walking,

And walking,

And walking.

Brown-orange specks paint the ground, rising up and down like waves. The glaring sun scalds my skin, turning it into a crisp mud-like color. Glass beads drip down my head and everything dances around, as if on fire. Every hour, my water decreases little by little until it's as empty as the desert. My throat feels like I've eaten sand.

I've got to keep on going.

But my legs won't let me. They bury themselves in the sand, refusing to move anymore. A glimmer screams from far away.

Water.

I crawl into the clear, freezing water. I drop into it, letting the cold embrace me as I grip a rock to prevent going downstream. I float on the water as it runs past me, my eyes closed.

A flash of light explodes in my head as a vision of a gun at Uncle's head ambushes me. I throw my eyelids open. If Bao finds out Uncle helped me escape...

"Don't think about this right now. He'll be fine. Uncle is Bao's assistant. He will never get rid of him because Bao knows it's the easy way out. He loves making you all suffer," The Voice remarks.

But I still can't help but worry. He's responsible for Hala's death.

"Worry about it after you're out of the country."

I pull myself out of the water, a sudden hot breeze hitting me. I lift myself up and continue walking, my muscles on fire.

BĀJĪSĪTĀN.

Pakistan.

Finally, after a month of walking, I'm free. I'm finally free.

My heart begins pounding and turns into ice. Tears gather at the brim of my eyes. I suck them back in and take the one step to be officially in Pakistan. A cloud of peace forms above me and rains down, washing all the cuts and bruises away. The chains tying me to China clink to the ground.

*"Shénme shì...*What are you doing," a deep voice booms behind me. I spin around, my eyes locking with the guard's. A furry mustache is plastered on his face and his head is completely barren of hair. His nose juts out like a cliff and his dark eyes search.

"What are you doing," he asks again.

"I'm entering Pakistan."

"ID?"

He holds his hand out.

"ID? What do you mean? I don't have an ID. I'm only sixteen."

"Where are your parents?"

"They...I...I don't have any."

"I can't let you in," he mumbles.

"W...Why?"

"You don't have proper identification. For all I know, you could be a criminal."

"I'm not a criminal. I'm an innocent child trying to get into a Muslim country. I'm a Uyghur. I've been kept in a camp for months and I finally managed to escape. I have to get away. Please."

His eyebrows arch and a tight line forms on his mouth. "You see that guard? Go to him. He'll help you."

I dart to the lone figure in the distance.

"Please, sir, you have to help me..."

As soon as he turns around, with a grim, smug smirk on his face, my heart rips apart, pounding so hard, my ribs crack. His deep scar gives it all away.

He's

The

"Superior."

33

OTUZ ÜCH

"PLEASE, SIR."

The “superior” lifts me off the ground.

"Now, I’ve finally got my hands on you. You can’t escape now."

"Please, sir. I'll be out of here within a second. I won't come back and I won't bother you or any other Han person again. Please."

"You do remember the *history* between us, right? You are the reason I’m out here rather than in Xinjiang, hunting the rest of your people. In case you haven’t realized, I serve my country faithfully. You Uyghurs are terrorists, *Xíngshì.* I won't let a criminal like you get away that easily. "

"I'll do anything. *Please,* sir."

"It is my duty as a Chinese citizen and guard to protect my homeland from the likes of you. It is my *new* job and I'm taking it very seriously. Imagine the reward I'll get for delivering a Uyghur escapee. I will never have to work again and then, I can finally get back at my ex-commander," he grins greedily.

Thwack.

I bury my foot into the man's stomach. He immediately drops me, clutching his stomach, a pain-ridden expression glued to his face.

"Run, run, *run,"* The Voice shrieks. My legs move like the wind, carrying me away. The guards shout but soon, they just become squeaks in the distance.

Suddenly the ground disappears.

"You're coming with me," the Pakistani guard orders.

"No. Let me go."

"Not a chance. You entered Pakistan illegally. You must be returned to where you came from," he replies, his voice rising.

"No. You can't send me back. *I. Can't. Go. Back.* "

"I'm sorry. It's the law."

"Please. Take me to your president. I can convince him."

“It's the law made *by* the government. You can't do anything about it."

"Then kill me. Please, do that much for me."

"I can't do that. What do you think I am? *A murderer?"* He yells, his face turning into a tomato.

"I think you're a *tyrant* along with your government. What kind of a person sends another human back to the killers he escaped from?"

Then I see it. The black box-like vehicle.

I see how cruel,
How heartless,
How ruthless
These people are.
They're
sending
me
back.

My heart goes limp and my entire body turns into ice. My head cracks from the pressure.

I'm thrown into the back of the black van.

I'm thrown back into the darkness.

I'm thrown back into the chains.

"Don't worry, this won't hurt a bit.," a sinister, deep voice chuckles.

"Do whatever you want, Chen. You've already taken everything. I don't have anything left."

Bzzzzzz.

I give up struggling.

I give up fighting.

I give up hoping until the darkness hungrily devours my broken soul.

HALA

KAZAKHSTAN NOW

34

OTUZ TÖT

KRRRRRR.

My mind buzzes with life and I stumble forward, crashing into a wall. Something is wrapped around me like a cocoon and my limbs are stuck.

I'm...moving? In a vehicle?

Grrrrmmm.

I roll backwards and hit something thin.

"Ow," someone sharply whispers.

The cloth hugging me slowly unwraps and I look up into the eyes of a guard.

I open my mouth to scream but he clamps his hand onto my mouth.

"Shhhh. It's okay. We're taking you to safety," he whispers.

Something glints in hand.

"I have to do this. It's for your protection."

He jams the object into my arm and within seconds, the world turns dark.

MY EYES FLUTTER open and a painful groan escapes my lips. My neck feels like it's been shut and a fire roars inside it.

I try to get up but something heavy is on top of me.

"She's awake," a deep, fuzzy voice bellows.

"Hurry and give her the medicine. We can't have her make any noise," a woman says.

"No. Don't. I'll be quiet," I croak.

The woman sighs. "Okay. Here." The woman takes the weight off me and sits me up. A cool liquid travels down my throat as she lifts the cup higher.

"Thank you."

"Shhhh. Now rest and don't make a sound, my daughter."

The woman rubs my arm, humming while the trees outside zoom past us.

Until everything freezes.

The car goes from moving to a stop.

The woman and her companion's eyes widen and they struggle to wrap a blanket around me. With a *thud,* heavy objects fall onto me until I can barely breathe.

Thump. Thump.

"Your passports?"

Thumpthump. Thumpthump.

"Here they are, sir."

THUMPTHUMP. THUMPTHUMP.

Passports?

A realization crashes into me.

They're taking me out of the country.

"How many of you are there?"

"Just us and the two people in the back, sir."

"You don't seem like tourists. Why are you going to Kazakhstan?"

"We're soldiers of the government, sir. We have been sent by officials from Xinjiang."

"Alright, you're all clear."

The car pants a few inches forward.

"Wait."

"Yes, sir?"

"I forgot to check your car. Open the trunk."

Krrrr.

The driver steps out and opens the trunk.

Scrrrr.

"Alright. Now open the door to the backseats."

The door near my head swings open.

Silence.

"What's that?"

A hand grips the object on top of me.

My blood grows cold.

"Rugs," the driver replies.

"Rugs?"

"Yes."

"Why would soldiers like you need rugs in Kazakhstan?"

"I have my own business and I sell rugs. I thought this would be a good business opportunity."

"May I see these *rugs?"*

"Of course."

The blanket is removed and as I lay, frozen in place, I see the man's intense eyes examining the rugs.

"Huh, these are really nice. Do you have a business card I may have for future reference? I would love to buy them."

"Here," the driver says.

"You're all free to go now."

"Thank you, sir."

Doors slam and then, the trees are zooming by once again. The rugs are taken off me and a gust of cool air blows into me. Beads of sweat drip down my face and my heart stops pounding.

I'm out of China.
I'm
finally
out
of
China.

As the world whizzes by, my mind drifts away and my eyes close, finally at peace.

35

OTUZ BESH

A CRACK OF white melts onto my eyes. As I force myself up, it spreads like a growing puddle until everything radiates color. My body sinks into the clouds as a heavy blanket rests on me.

...

Clouds? Blanket?

I shoot up, my eyes taking everything in and I tumble out of the bed, stumbling onto the floor. My entire body feels tight and I rub my sore back. I breathe a heavy sigh of relief and close my eyes, taking in the silence.

Creeeeak.

A ghost-like woman peers through the door and her empty eyes reflect the same spirit they did long ago. Her face is a light gray while the folds under her eyes are black. Her lips are slightly ajar, revealing a few black gaps.

Tears flood into my eyes and my breath scratches against my throat.

"Mama."

The sun looks down upon us and smiles, showering us with its warm, calm light.

It's all over.

It's all over.

It's all over.

The tears pour out in rivers, taking the nightmares of torture,

Pain,

And humiliation with them.

I cry until there are no tears left.

I cry until my mind empties of

Every

Single

Nightmare.

"Hala," Mama croaks as her wet face glimmers in the sunlight, "Hala?"

"Where have you been, Mama? Where have you been?"

"I didn't know where you were. I couldn't look for you. I had to leave. I'm sorry. I'm sorry." She sobs, red cracking her eyes.

"You were there one second and gone the next."

She hands me a stained piece of paper and my eyes glide over the words.

To Hala's mom,

We pray you are safe in Kazakhstan and that Hala reaches you safely. Unfortunately, we can't explain everything in detail but we managed to get a hold of Hala's "body" through a sympathetic guard. From there, she was transported to you. We know these are unusual circumstances but once you have read this message, burn it. We hope both of you will live peacefully, away from the Chinese government.

I look up and meet Mama's eyes.

"I'm so, so grateful these people were there. I'm so grateful I can see you again."

"Where's Papa?"

"They...they killed him," she pauses for a moment, "Where's Ürkesh?"

"I don't know," the tears drip harder at the mention of his name. Everything spirals away and I'm back in the camp.

"Stop it."

"Make me."

"Stop it. She's coming with me."

"Too bad. Take her from me. Come on. Take her."

"Stop. Stop. Stop. Stop. Stop. Stop. Stop. Stopstopstopstop."

"Ürkesh. Ürkesh. Ürkesh. Ürkesh. Ürkesh. Ürkesh."

I fall back into reality. It was just a flashback.

My heart pounds against my chest like a drummer beating his drum.

THUMPTHUMPTHUMP.

"Hala? Hala?"

"Yes?"

"Where is he?"

"I don't know."

"Isn't he supposed to be with you? Didn't you escape with him?" panic echoes in her voice. She breaks down, collapsing onto the wood floor, a pool forming around her.

"What's wrong, Mama?"

"He wouldn't have spared him. He wouldn't have spared him," she whispers.

"What do you mean?"

"He wouldn't have spared him."

"Who wouldn't have spared Ürkesh?"

"Chen."

"Who's Chen?"

"His father," she mutters.

"W...What?"

"Chen would never have spared Ürkesh."

"Mama, what's going on? Who's Chen?"

She sits up, searching my eyes. When she can't find what she's looking for, she casts her eyes down and a tear rolls down her cheek.

"When I was young, a man named Chen forced me to marry him. From that marriage, Ürkesh was born. I escaped him after that. Chen has been after your brother ever since."

"But...Isn't Papa Ürkesh's father?"

"No. He isn't."

"Does Ürkesh know?"

"No," a sudden sadness blankets her eyes as they grow cloudy and rain salty tears.

BZZZZZZ.

"Hala, can you take the phone? My hands are dirty."

"Hello?"

"Hala, come back to China this instant. You belong here, not in some foreign country. Do you realize how bad you're making our country look? Come back here before the government has to drag you out of there. Now, you aren't a threat to China anymore but to the whole world."

I smash the phone into its stand, my lungs clawing for air.

"Hala?" Mama asks, peering from behind the wall.

"It was Uncle. He's threatening us. They're making him. We're not safe here."

"We can't, Hala. This is the safest place."

"The government has found us. They're coming. If we don't leave now, we might regret it."

"I'll try to contact someone tomorrow. Okay?"

I nod, my blood still ice.

"MAMA?"

I stick my head into her bedroom and walk towards the bed.

Silence.

Only rumpled sheets greet me. I creep to the kitchen but not a single dish has been touched.

Cree.

My eyes bulge out of their sockets. The front door is wide open, the wind rushing into the house.

"Mama? Mama? Mama?"

I race through the house. The air grows heavy. I dart out the front door, my eyes scanning the crowds.

Crash.

"Oh, I'm sorry," a tall boy mutters.

My mind erupts.

"Ürkesh? Ürkesh? Ürkesh?"

I throw my arms around him but they only meet the still air.

Whoosh.

A slightly crumpled paper glides onto the road. I unfold the crisp, thick sheet and drink the black ink.

YOU'RE NEXT

Where Hala and her
mother reunite

Kazakhstan

From where Ürkesh
is sent back

Pakistan

Chen’s Camp

Bao’s Camp

China

N

W

E

P

S

AUTHOR'S NOTE

"We do not have to accept the world as we find it.
And we have a responsibility to leave our world a better place
and never walk by on the other side of injustice."
-Ed Miliband

Endangered is a historical fiction novel. However, the extent of discrimination and genocide against the Uyghurs and other Turkic minorities is real and happening as you are reading this. It is a horrifying yet unknown reality to many.

The Uyghurs are an ethnically Turkic people that live in Kazakhstan, Kyrgyzstan and northwest China. Northwestern China is known as East Turkestan to the Uyghurs and Xinjiang to the Chinese. Around 2014, tensions began between the Turkic people and the Chinese Communist Party (CCP). This led to the construction of "re-education" camps, otherwise known as concentration camps. Anything could get a Uyghur there. Growing a beard, praying, talking in their language; all the things we take for granted.

In these camps, the Uyghurs are forced to assimilate to Han Chinese culture and are not allowed to express their own religion or culture. If they do express any component of their culture or religion, they are beaten and tortured.

The CCP also forces Uyghurs to make products for them, otherwise known as slavery. Companies like Nike, Apple, Samsung, Sketchers and 80 others have been found to use forced labor to cheaply produce their merchandise.

It is impossible to summarize my research in a page or two so I encourage you to research the facts and testimonies yourself.

What makes this conflict different is that the perpetrator is the CCP, an economic leader of the world. Between 15 to 20 percent of world trade comes from China. If you look through your home, you'll find that most products are made in China. So if the US or any other country is to do something about the Uyghur genocide, they would be harming their economy because China would have an incentive to cut trade with that country.

The CCP is betraying the Turkic people and the world. They are breaking every single word in the Genocide Convention, which they have signed and the world is doing nothing. China is masking what is truly happening inside Xinjiang. Imagine having security cameras watching your every move. Or your biodata being collected. Or worrying that the police will break down your door anytime. Or that one of your loved ones will disappear forever. We take safety and freedom for granted. We take religious and cultural freedom for granted. We take the fact that we sleep at night peacefully for granted.

The Uyghurs don't have that blessing. They live in constant fear and terror. They watch as their families and neighbors disappear, never heard from again.

I hope that by reading *Endangered,* you will gain awareness of this horrifying genocide. Spread this book and the history it contains. Stop buying products made from enslavement. The Uyghurs have been silenced so let's be their voice.

Together, we can save an endangered nation.

Kian Sabik

THE NEXT FEW PAGES CONTAIN IMAGES. PLEASE TAKE CAUTION AS SOME IMAGES MAY BE DISTURBING

City in Xinjiang
Source: Piqsels

Minaret Of A Mosque in Kashgar
Source: iStock

Nomadic Settlement in Xinjiang
Source: Piqsels

Camel Herd In Xinjiang

Source: Piqsels

Urumqi, Xinjiang

Source: Piqsels

Uyghur Boy Eating Traditional Food

Source: iStock

Police Escorting A Prisoner

Source: xinjiangpolicefiles.org

Detainees In A Camp

Source: xinjiangpolicefiles.org

Prisoners Undergoing Abuse

Source: xinjiangpolicefiles.org

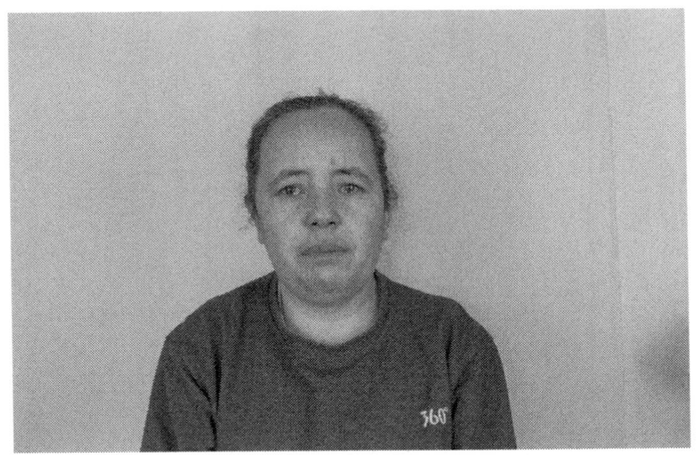

Hawagul Tewekkul

Location and Reason For Internment Unknown

Source: xinjiangpolicefiles.org

ACKNOWLEDGEMENTS

As deeply rewarding as it has been, writing a novel is more challenging than I could've imagined, and it wouldn't have been possible without so many people by my side. First and foremost, I'm so grateful to God for putting the idea in my heart and giving me the strength to work toward this cause. I would also like to thank everyone who helped this idea become a reality from the bottom of my heart. Special thanks to:

All my family for your immense support and encouragement.

Mom and Dad for being the most incredible supporters throughout the process. It wasn't easy and I love you for always standing by my side.

My sweet sister for your thorough feedback and for your help shaping my book to the final version.

My little brother for sharing your excitement and constant motivation.

R Santamaria for your inspiring quotes & A Cortinas for cheering me on. Thank you both for your excitement, support and time.

M Baajour, A Mamun & M Yousef for spreading the word and helping me with this cause.

S Malilk, O Qaroot and all supporters of my Launchgood campaign.

My beta reader, bushelofwatermelon, for your feedback and suggestions. They have been extremely valuable to this story.

My cover designer from Ebook Launch for turning my book cover ideas into a reality.

My editor, W Muruli, for editing my book on such short notice.

And last but not least, you, my valuable reader. Thank you for reading my novel. I hope you were able to experience the Uyghurs' lives in Xinjiang. Please join my cause by spreading the word and reviewing my work. It would mean a lot.

ABOUT THE AUTHOR

Kian Sabik's secluded workspace is her refuge from a complex world. Having a passion for intellectual pursuits, Kian finds comfort in reading and writing, sailing between tales of the past and present. When not drawn into a world of words, Kian loves traveling, bike riding, playing chess, sparring, and listening to her favorite podcasts. If you want to find out when Kian's next book will come out, follow her on Instagram at @kian.sabik

Made in the USA
Middletown, DE
09 September 2022

72769073R00179